"I'll let you go on one condition."

"What?"

"One kiss."

She glanced at him but then quickly looked away.

"Look, we'll never see each other again and I want to finish this evening having kissed a beautiful woman who's made me feel more real than I have in a long time."

Her alarm had quickly given way to excitement. "But you hardly know me."

"Somehow I feel I do." He lowered his voice. "Please."

She should've said no and left, but she wasn't going to. One kiss. She'd never see him again and she didn't want to miss this opportunity.

Anna Marie seized his hand. "No one can see us," she whispered as she led him to a small storage closet and closed the door behind them. She turned to face him. "Okay, now—"

Books by Dara Girard

Kimani Romance

Sparks
The Glass Slipper Project
Taming Mariella
Power Play
A Gentleman's Offer
Body Chemistry

DARA GIRARD

is an award-winning author of both fiction and nonfiction books. She enjoys writing romance because of the range it provides, from comedy to suspense. Her novels are known for their sense of humor, interesting plot twists and witty dialogue.

In addition to writing novels, Dara enjoys reading, painting and going for long drives.

Dara loves hearing from her readers. You can contact her at www.daragirard.com, or P.O. Box 10345, Silver Spring, Maryland 20914.

ROUND the CLOCK

DARA GIRARD

KIMANI™
ROMANCE

To those who believe in dreaming big.

KIMANI PRESS™

Recycling programs
for this product may
not exist in your area.

ISBN-13: 978-0-373-86122-4

ROUND THE CLOCK

www.kimanipress.com

Printed in U.S.A.

Dear Reader,

Welcome to the fourth book in THE BLACK STOCKINGS SOCIETY series.

Have you ever wanted something so bad you'd do nearly anything to get it? That's the question Anna Marie Williams faces when she gets a chance to meet and seduce her high-school crush, bad-boy Desmond Rockwell. Fortunately, Desmond is willing to be seduced and has a few moves of his own. However, there's a snag….

A big one.

But with the help of the Black Stockings Society, Anna Marie realizes that getting the man of your dreams is one thing, but keeping him is something else—something worth fighting for.

I hope you enjoy Anna Marie and Desmond's story.

You can find out more about this series and learn about my other titles on my Web site, www.daragirard.com.

All the best,

Dara Girard

Acknowledgments
Many thanks to my editor Glenda Howard, Kelli Martin
and the rest of the Kimani Press team for helping me
make this series a reality.

Chapter 1

More than anything in the world, Anna Marie Williams wanted two things: 1) to tell her boss to shut up and 2) a night with Desmond Rockwell. However, she knew the latter was impossible and the former merely wishful thinking. Instead she sat and listened to her boss, Sandy "the Cobra" Martin, inside a cramped office whose view offered nothing but the sight of another equally ugly brick building like theirs. She glanced at a pigeon perched on the windowsill as a harsh wind ruffled its feathers, giving no sign that winter had passed and it was now spring. The wind threatened to push the bird off its ledge, but it remained unmoved.

Anna Marie mirrored the bird as she sat composed in her crisp gray suit, her sharp brown eyes serene while Sandy shouted at her.

"You are the most worthless employee I've ever had," she said, her booming voice making the room feel even smaller. Stacks of boxes surrounded her desk and file cabinets, evidence of Sandy's addiction to Internet shopping. "If I could hire a tree stump to do your job I would."

Anna Marie blinked with boredom and stared across the desk at her boss as though Sandy were talking about the weather instead of her incompetence. "Ms. Martin—"

Sandy slapped her hand on the desk, snapping off one of her fake pink nails. She didn't notice as it flew across the room. "I don't care what your excuse is." She tapped a stack of papers. "How the hell did this happen? You're paid to make sure that *nothing* leaves this office without being thoroughly checked."

"I know."

"You know?" Sandy said with a sneer. "Personally, I don't think you know a damn thing. This could have gone out and been printed. Do I have to do everything around here?" She threw her hands up in the air exasperated. "I'm surrounded by morons." She narrowed her gaze. "I'm not happy. And when I'm not happy I make other people's lives miserable." She turned her chair to the window.

Anna Marie stifled a yawn, used to Sandy's

dramatic displays. Even when Sandy was happy she was miserable. She hadn't developed the nickname the Cobra for nothing. She could strike at any time and Anna Marie was used to her venomous tongue. Few things about Sandy were real—not her nails, her hair color or her chin. Anna Marie remembered Sandy when she didn't have one. She used to be a secretary before she slept with and blackmailed the right executive to get her present position.

Anna Marie didn't judge her strategy; she just wished that getting a management position would have made her happy. Instead she'd become a micromanaging tyrant in a four-person office in the Virginia Department of Health and Human Services's human resources department. They were information specialists. It was a government job and while the pay was not significant, the benefits were great. Anna Marie's job wasn't exciting but despite this, she performed well.

She was responsible for editing and rewriting publications and reports written by other agency staff within HR to ensure that all grammar and punctuation were correct and appropriate for the intended audience. Twice a year Anna Marie worked closely with her coworker, Nancy Helm, to prepare HHS's biannual and annual reports. She looked at the papers on Sandy's desk with regret. She'd put Nancy in charge of layout and cross-referencing, but again, her coworker had fallen short. Unfortunately, Sandy had seen it before Anna Marie could cover for her. But as always, Anna Marie took the blame.

"You're not listening to a word I'm saying," Sandy snapped.

"Of course I am," Anna Marie replied in a soft voice that only made Sandy's frown increase.

"You're pathetic." She leaned back in her chair. "I'm the only one who knows how to get things done around here…."

Anna Marie glanced at her watch as Sandy continued her tirade, wondering how long she would keep her. Sometimes her rants would last half an hour and cut in to her lunch break. Her coworkers trembled in Sandy's presence, but to Anna Marie, Sandy's behavior was nothing new. She was used to abuse. Her parents had called her worse things and used their fists to emphasize their displeasure; Child Protective Services took her and her sister away.

Her first foster parents said she was stupid, her second told her she was ugly, her third that she was useless and her fourth that she'd never amount to anything. Then she'd met Mrs. Bell. Thankfully, she was her last placement. She was the fifth and the best and everything would have been perfect if Anna Marie hadn't run away.

"I hope I've made myself clear." Sandy shoved

the stack of papers across the table. "Make it shine or else."

Anna Marie started to smile, wanting to call her bluff—Sandy would never risk firing her—but instead said, "I will."

"You will what?"

"I will, Ms. Martin."

"Good. Now get out."

Anna Marie stood, eager to leave. Suddenly Sandy swore. "Wait," she bellowed, looking in horror at her extended right hand. "I lost a nail. Nancy!"

Nancy appeared in the doorway looking like a scared mouse. "Yes, Ms. Martin?"

"Help me find my nail."

Nancy immediately fell to her knees and started looking despite the fact that she was wearing a red rayon skirt that would get filthy on the dirty floor.

"Where are you going?" Sandy shouted when Anna Marie began to leave.

Anna Marie motioned to the papers in her hand. "I have work to do."

"You can do it later. You're not that busy. I know what you do. Help Nancy look. I have a meeting this afternoon."

Anna Marie opened her mouth to argue then caught Nancy's anxious expression and closed it. She briefly scanned the floor, then saw the pink nail in the far corner. She walked over to it and crushed it under her heel, then picked up the ruined remains and placed them on Sandy's desk. "Now I'll get back to work."

Anna Marie returned to her desk and with a weary sigh rested the document on a side table. She turned to her computer and retrieved the electronic file and began making corrections.

Nancy popped up from behind the partition. "I saw what you did," she said. "Fortunately, the Cobra didn't."

"Yes, that was the point," Anna Marie said without looking up.

"Pretty bold of you. Especially since she has that important meeting this afternoon and wants to look her best."

"Not really. She stashes extra nails in her desk drawer."

Nancy's eyes widened. "Really?"

"Yes."

Nancy bit her lip. Anna Marie stifled a groan because Nancy only did that when she felt guilty. And she had every reason to. She was totally unsuited to her job. She had been a housewife until her husband of twenty years decided to remarry and start a new family, leaving Nancy, who had few administrative skills, with a son in high school and a daughter in college. Nancy was an attractive, impeccably dressed woman in her forties who could have looked younger if stress hadn't made her pale skin dry and patchy. "Are you okay?" she asked.

Anna Marie continued to type. "I'm fine."

"We could hear her screaming all the way down the hall." She lowered her voice. "Thanks for covering for me. I don't know how you can take it. She always makes me cry."

Anna Marie shrugged. She couldn't remember the last time she'd cried. "I've endured worse. She doesn't bother me."

"Did you tell her I did it?"

Anna Marie looked up at her, trying to be patient. "Has she called you into her office?"

"I'm really sorry. It won't happen again."

Anna Marie forced a smile, knowing that it would, but said nothing. She didn't want to discourage her.

Nancy disappeared behind her partition then reappeared. "The girls from the other department and I are going for Friday-night drinks later. Would you like to come?"

"I'm busy, but thanks." Anna Marie didn't have friends—never had. She found it better that way, but it seemed Nancy was determined to try and be one.

"Well, if you change your mind, we'll be at The Hub until late."

Anna Marie smiled to soften Nancy's disappointment. "Okay."

She continued typing, waiting for Nancy to disappear again, but instead her coworker wheeled her chair around the corner. "I wish you'd give me a chance to thank you for all your help," Nancy said in a pleading tone.

"You've already thanked me. That's enough."

"But it doesn't feel like enough. I know I'm no good at this job, but you've made it work for me. I would have lost everything if it hadn't been for you. I needed this job. The hours and the perks are wonderful. I don't know what I'd do if I lost it."

Anna Marie nodded. Nancy was right. The perks were worth the hassle of tolerating the Cobra and Anna Marie prided herself on doing a good job. Her reports were always perfect, always on time. But since Nancy's hire six months ago, Anna Marie had seen her job record slipping and knew she would soon have to do something about it. She didn't know what, but she wouldn't abandon Nancy. She had a soft spot in her heart for the timid, sweet-natured woman.

If the Cobra would let Nancy take time off for two key workshops, she knew Nancy would learn some essential skills needed for her position, but she knew this would not happen. The Cobra treasured her job too much to educate her subordinates for fear that they would one day usurp her. "I only helped a little bit." Before Nancy could argue further, Anna Marie said, "You'd better get back to your desk before the Cobra leaves her den."

Nancy's face blanched and she wheeled away in her office chair.

Anna Marie worked until seven that evening, then went home ready to relax. She stopped in front of her apartment and for a moment let herself imagine that Desmond Rockwell was inside waiting for her. But that dream always died the moment she opened the door. Tonight was no different. When she opened the door to her apartment, she was met with a foul odor. She covered her nose and mouth then glanced at her boyfriend, Bruno Delane, who sat on the couch—his favorite position since he'd quit his job and decided to become a consultant. She still wasn't sure what he did. He was reasonably handsome and fit—if one could ignore the slight paunch that stretched his *Virginia Is for Lovers* T-shirt.

He was certainly no Desmond Rockwell, but to be fair, Desmond had aged extremely well in her imagination. She'd last seen him when she was eighteen and she had no idea what the years may have done to him. She didn't care; to her Desmond would always be the handsome bad boy with a wicked smile who had stolen her heart.

"Welcome home, babe," Bruno said.

Anna Marie removed her gaze from him and surveyed the room. "What is that awful smell?" She had a sinking feeling that Bruno had been in the kitchen, which always proved to be a disaster. When it came to cooking, Bruno had as much finesse as a jellyfish trying to cross a highway. He'd once set fire to a dishcloth while trying to boil an egg.

He took a sip of his beer and shrugged. "Oh, does it still smell? I must have gotten used to it," he said and returned his gaze to their wide-screen TV.

"Gotten used to what?"

He motioned to the kitchen. "I burnt something in the oven. How come you didn't leave anything for dinner?"

Anna Marie took off her jacket. "I've been busy."

"You know I hate coming home to nothing to eat."

I didn't realize you'd left. "There are leftovers."

"I ate leftovers for lunch. I'm not going to have them again for dinner." He took another swig of his beer.

Anna Marie left her things by the door and headed for the kitchen. "I'll start cooking now."

"Never mind. I ordered something."

She stopped, dread now mingled with uneasiness. "What did you order?"

"Calzones."

"I hate them," she mumbled. To her, calzones were like eating an oversize pizza meat pie. She hated meat pies.

"What?"

She adjusted some live flowers she had on an oak table in the foyer. "Nothing."

He sat up, his voice hurt. "I heard you. You said you hate them. I'm trying my best to please you. I find nothing in the house and I order dinner and you tell me that you hate it?"

"I'm sorry. I know you forgot." *As always.* Anna Marie went into the kitchen. Dirty dishes lined the counter and others sat stacked in the sink along with a dirty dishcloth. She opened the oven and saw the blackened food that had spilled over and looked as if it had exploded.

"You didn't clean up," she said, taking hold of her gag reflex. What had he been trying to cook? It smelled like old broccoli and rotten eggs.

He crumpled his beer can and set it aside. "I'll get to it, babe, don't worry."

Anna Marie sighed and pulled on a pair of plastic gloves. She cleaned the oven, washed the dishes, wiped down the countertop, then began preparing something—he'd have to eat the calzone alone. As the chicken baked, Anna Marie sat at their dining table and went through her mail. She ripped open a bill, saw the amount owed and groaned. She looked at Bruno, whose position hadn't changed since she'd arrived home, and waved the bill.

"You bought a new portable hard drive?"

Their apartment was small so he barely had to look at her to see what she was waving. "I'll pay you back."

Anna Marie shoved the bill back in the envelope in disgust. Bruno's overspending kept them in debt. She heard the timer go off in the kitchen and stood. "Dinner's ready."

Bruno jumped to his feet at the sound of his two favorite words. He stretched then followed her into the kitchen. "Hmm, smells good. But I told you I'd ordered dinner."

She moved around him and grabbed a pair of oven mitts from a drawer. "You can save the calzones for your lunch."

He nodded. "That's a good idea. How was your day?" he asked as she handed him a plate.

"Fine."

"Are you mad at me because of the credit charge?"

She pulled the chicken from the oven and rested it on the counter. "No."

He moved behind her and put his hand on her bottom. "I can make it up to you in many ways."

Anna Marie moved away. "Yes, but unfortunately, I can't put *that* in the bank."

He pressed against her and whispered in her ear. "Baby, you're my bank and I'd like to make a deposit."

She took his plate from him and loaded it with food. "I'm busy tonight."

He frowned. "Doing what?"

She put gravy on his potatoes.

"Oh, that stupid book club?" he said in disgust.

Anna Marie handed him his dinner then began making her own plate. "Yes. That."

Bruno set his plate down on the counter and folded his arms. "You prefer those women to me?"

"You can answer that question as you watch me drive away." She cut off a piece of chicken and put it on her plate.

He scowled. "What's that supposed to mean?"

Anna Marie silently swore. She had to watch her mouth. It had gotten her in trouble before and she didn't want to put Bruno in a bad mood. She lightened her voice and softened her face into a smile. "It means that's why I've made your favorite dish. So that you won't miss me. Come on, let's eat."

He drew her close. "You're sure you're not mad at me?"

"No, I'm not mad. Careful of my plate," she warned, balancing it over his head.

"I'm not hungry." He kissed her neck. "Are you?"

She was starving. Anna Marie looked at the kitchen clock and knew she had a few minutes to indulge him, but didn't feel in the mood. She looked at him and a part of her wanted to say, "It's not working, let's break up," but although she'd silently practiced the words many times, she never spoke them and doubted she ever would. The best way to deal with Bruno was distraction.

"If you don't eat your dinner, you can't get dessert. I made your favorite." She'd baked a peach cobbler two days earlier and had kept it hidden in the back of their refrigerator.

Bruno stared at her and she could see his mind

working—food or a quickie? There was no contest. "Let's eat."

An hour later, Anna Marie sped down the road swearing. Bruno had enjoyed dinner and dessert and she hadn't rushed him. She knew she had to keep him in a good mood so that he'd never suspect what she was really up to or who she really was.

She parked in the back of The Palace of Sin, the adult entertainment club where she worked, and dashed to the employee entrance.

"What's the rush?" Fred, the manager, said.

"Sorry I'm late."

He glanced at his watch. "Late? You're early. Come on, you've got to see this crowd." He gently tugged on her arm and took her into the executive lounge. She had no fear of being discovered because people usually didn't notice her. The Palace of Sin was an upscale men's club decorated in an Eastern décor. The stage resembled a sheikh's palace with heavy velvet curtains, embroidered pillows with gold thread and rare stones, tall solid brass candlesticks and brightly colored silk scarves. Before the night was over, Anna Marie would use all four.

She glanced up at the lighting to make sure it was in the right position. Then her gaze fell on the crowd. A large group of men in suits and some in casual wear sat at several round tables decorated with candles and plenty of food and drinks.

"Do you like the arrangement?" Fred asked.

"It's perfect."

"Have you changed your mind?"

"No." She started to turn, then stopped as though someone had struck her. Two men had entered the room. The first was a regular. He always dressed in a tailored double-breasted suit as though he were visiting the president or some foreign dignitary. He kept his mustache trim and his shoes polished, which was in stark contrast to his companion. The other man wore jeans and a black leather jacket and looked like he could start a bar fight and win with little effort. The second man moved with casual, masculine elegance. He wasn't a regular, but she knew him.

A jolt of awareness seized her and for a few minutes she wasn't sure she could breathe. Even at a distance she could see every angle of his face. She knew the look and color of his eyes, the shape of his mouth and his lips. Her mind whispered his name, Desmond Rockwell, and her eyes drank him up. Seeing him again was like one of her dreams and she didn't want to wake. She watched him make his way through the crowd—a tall, dark, mysterious figure who caused Anna Marie to remember all the pain and pleasure of her past.

"That man has never been here before," she said, trying to keep her voice neutral, although her heart raced.

"No, he's with Mr. Advent."

"Put them up front. I want them to have the best seat in the house."

Fred looked at her, startled. "Are you sure?"

"Fred, this is my last night. I want it to be memorable."

He reluctantly motioned to the hostess. "If that's what you think you want."

Anna Marie glanced at Desmond once more. "I know exactly what I want."

Chapter 2

Desmond Rockwell glanced around the club with a critical look of boredom, wondering how he'd been convinced to come. Then he looked over at his friend and client Julius Advent and knew why. He'd do anything to keep Advent happy, even this.

Julius unbuttoned his jacket. "You're going to love this."

"This really isn't my thing."

"It will be tonight. You don't know how hard it was to get tickets. This is her last performance. The moment you see her dance, you're going to thank me."

"Right," he said, doubtful. Desmond wasn't

against exotic dancers, but he preferred a different type of entertainment. He and Julius started to walk toward a free table when a woman in a tight black dress stepped in front of them. "Excuse me, gentlemen, but you've been selected to sit in our special seats. Please follow me."

Desmond turned to his friend. Julius shoved him forward. "Just go."

They followed the woman to a table situated directly in front of the stage. Once they were seated, she draped a silk scarf around their necks. "Compliments of Malika. Enjoy."

Julius could barely contain his excitement. "Front-row seats. Can you believe this?"

Desmond tugged on the scarf. "What's this for?"

"It's Malika's signature." Julius raised his hand for two drinks. "Tonight's going to change your life."

Anna Marie emerged from behind a screen in her dressing room as Malika—the best-known dancer at The Palace of Sin for the last ten years. She wore a long, wavy black wig, her body encased in a silken harem costume. She made some final adjustments, then looked at herself in the full-length mirror off to the side.

Belinda, another dancer at the club, stared at her, impressed. "Those men are toast. When did you buy that?"

"I didn't," Anna Marie said, feeling free to be

honest with her. Belinda was the only other person besides Fred who knew who she really was. Anna Marie had helped her get the position at the club years ago when Belinda was forced to dance in a dingy bar. Since helping her, Belinda had become a trusted colleague. "I had it made to order. I found this quaint fabric store and the store manager picked out several pieces for me, took my measurements and had it custom-fitted."

"It's more than custom-fitted. It looks like it's your skin."

Anna Marie grinned. "Those were my instructions." She stared at her image again. The store owner had helped her select a variety of exquisitely colorful silks and sheer fabrics and created a made-to-order, sexy, five-piece Arabian harem costume. It included a dark half-face veil revealing only her eyes, long detachable sleeves, a bejeweled bra top—that matched the exotic sandals she wore—sheer pants with silver coin trim and a thong.

Her jewelry consisted of several toe rings, an ankle bracelet and a 24k-gold amulet with earrings, which were the last items she'd put on. Anna Marie draped a sexy, floor-length sheer cover-up over her shoulders then sat in front of the vanity mirror to put on her makeup. She began outlining her eyes with a dark pencil.

"How was your evening?" Anna Marie asked, glancing at Belinda's hot-pink three-piece outfit.

"Once you're finished, you should be ready to go home." Anna Marie didn't understand why Belinda always stayed after her shift to be with her.

"And miss you dance? Never. I'm still learning."

"You're good."

Belinda glanced into her own mirror. "Maybe, but you're the best. And you get the best crowds, too." She turned to Anna Marie. "So, do you have a target tonight?"

"Maybe."

"I know you gave your signature to a new man."

Anna Marie shrugged. "It's fun."

Belinda stared at her for a moment, then said, "Are you sure you want to do this?"

She wished people would stop asking her that question. She knew it was the right thing. Tonight had to be her last performance. She'd had doubts about her decision before but knew it was time: Time to stop before she was caught. She'd managed to make a name for herself as Malika and a lot of money by dancing, but she didn't want her true identity ever revealed. It was time to move on.

She filled in her eyebrows. "Yes."

"We're all going to miss you," Belinda said in a teary voice. She grabbed her handbag and pulled out a tissue.

Strangely, Anna Marie knew she'd miss them. Her career had started innocently enough. After leaving Mrs. Bell, she'd wandered until getting her first job as a waitress in a club by lying about her age. Then she lied about her experience and started getting small gigs as a dancer and soon those jobs grew and Malika became a star. And for the past ten years, Anna Marie got to be someone totally different at night.

Belinda threw the tissue away and pulled a little black book out of her handbag. "Are you stopping 'cause of Bruno?"

It was one of the reasons. Keeping him in the dark was getting tricky. Anna Marie applied a bright red lipstick. "No."

Belinda took out a pen and began scribbling something down in her book. "When are you going to tell him what you do?"

"You mean *did*. And the answer is never. After tonight no one will ever know."

Belinda sent her a worried look. "Are you ashamed?"

Anna Marie set down her lipstick.

"We're not strippers," Belinda said. "We're dancers and this is an upscale place. Plus, you're one of the best."

"Thank you," Anna Marie said humbly, although she knew it to be true. She'd been featured in discreet male magazines and had two bestselling dance videos to prove it, but she also knew it was time for this part of her life to end.

"Even if you don't want to tell him, I think you should dump him."

Anna Marie turned to her stunned. "What?"

"From everything you've told me about him, he sounds like a real bore. Do you know how many men out there want you?"

"They want Malika," she said, smoothing out her wig. "Not Anna Marie. You know that."

Belinda shook her head. "But you're both."

"No. I'm one person by day and someone different by night. That's what has worked for me and it's not going to change."

"Yes, it is. Malika's quitting."

Anna Marie adjusted her veil. "Malika is retiring." She stood and stretched. "You have a good man. I take what I can get."

Belinda scribbled more notes in her black book. "You can get better."

"Hmm."

She snapped the book closed. "And you deserve better."

Anna Marie stared at the book, curious. "What were you writing?"

Belinda tucked the book back in her handbag. "Just ideas for my next performance."

Fred peeked his head in. "Two minutes. It's a full house."

Anna Marie smiled. "I'm ready. Let's go."

* * *

Desmond sipped his drink and tapped a beat on the table while Julius flirted with a waitress. Suddenly, the lights dimmed, indicating the show was about to begin. Desmond took one large swallow of his drink and was about to signal for another one when the room went dark.

The heavy curtains parted and on the stage a screen projected the image of desert sands and a twilight sky. Then a swirl of smoke filled the stage and a figure emerged: A beautiful woman in flowing, colorful silk. The music began to play and the woman moved her body to it as though she and the music were one. Desire and fire seemed to drive her movements. She captured the audience—mesmerizing them as though she were a snake charmer or a sorceress. She was a master of the light and smoke that surrounded her. She moved around the stage using the candles and curtains in erotic ways he didn't know were possible. She was in control and he was one of her captives.

Desmond felt a jolt of arousal he didn't expect. And before he could dampen it, the woman began to speak in a whisper as though talking only to him, her voice soft like the silk around his neck. "Do you want me? Because I want you."

She moved to the edge of the stage, her eyes meeting his. "Do you feel me touching you?" Her gaze went down his body and he felt his chest tighten.

"We are alone and I move only for you. Love me."
She moved away then danced as though being
embraced by a lover. She moved as if she were the
embodiment of sin, temptation and wanton desire.
She moved her hips, her arms, her chest—each
movement an invitation and a warning. The softness
of her flesh moved with precision to the beat and
rhythm of the music, undulating in a hypnotic manner
that held him hostage.

Desmond gripped his hands into fists, determined to meet her gaze. She again danced to the
edge of the stage, then grabbed the end of his scarf
and pulled it toward her, turning so it wrapped
around her waist, but he grabbed the end before it
completely left him.

For a moment she looked startled then she spun
out of the scarf and wrapped it again around his
neck, her hand brushing against his face. It took all
his control not to move. "My love, my master," she
whispered. "I am your slave." She drew away and
shimmered and spun, dancing as though she were
the air—something he could feel, but never touch.

Suddenly she stopped and the lights went dark.
When they came back on, the stage was empty.
Thunderous applause followed. Desmond barely
heard it, his heart and his head pounding. Where
was she? Who was she? What had just happened?

"Malika! Malika!" the crowd shouted.

The sultry figure came back onto the stage and

bowed, then blew them a kiss. She looked directly at Desmond and winked, then turned and the curtains closed.

Julius pounded the table. "Didn't I tell you she was fantastic?"

"Who is she?"

"Malika."

"No, in real life."

"Nobody knows. Shame this is her last performance."

Desmond turned to him, startled. "What?"

"I told you that this was her final performance. Why do you think I brought you?"

"I have to find out who she is."

"Leave it alone, Rockwell. Trust me, most of us have tried."

"I can't leave it," Desmond said in a tight voice. "There's something about her."

"Don't fall for that 'she danced for me' stuff. That's what she's paid to do. It's what she's good at." He picked up a candle. "These have speakers in them and she wears a tiny microphone so you can hear her talking. She makes you feel as though she's talking to you. She's made every man in this room think she's danced for him alone." Julius took off his scarf and laid it on the table. "It's a nice fantasy."

Desmond lifted the end of his scarf and inhaled the scent of her perfume. "It wasn't a fantasy. It was real."

Chapter 3

Anna Marie sat in front of her vanity mirror, not knowing whether she wanted to laugh, cry or faint. She'd danced for Desmond Rockwell. She had captured his attention and felt his gaze cascading over her body. His gaze had been intimate, intense and smoldering with lust. His name whispered in her mind as though he'd called out to her. Desmond Rockwell: Her first love and her first heartbreak. He had watched her as though she belonged to him. As though her body was his alone—his possession. She had sought to seek his surrender as she had done with most men, but he was stronger than that.

He was a sorcerer immune to her magic with a power that rivaled her own.

"Are you okay?" Belinda asked her as she entered the room.

Anna Marie grabbed her bottled water. "I'm fine. It was just a bit hot in there."

"Hot? Honey, it was steaming. You made a lot of men very happy."

"Then I've done my job."

"Don't let him rattle you."

Anna Marie turned to her. "Who?"

"That man. Your target. I've never seen a man look at you like that."

"Like what?"

Belinda rested a hand on her hip and flashed a sly grin. "As though he planned to own you."

Anna Marie laughed and twisted the cap back on her bottle. "That's the whole idea. Let him think that."

"I'd be careful."

"Why?"

"You danced as though you *wanted* him to own you."

"You're imagining things. I'm with Bruno, remember?"

"Yes, just be careful."

Anna Marie stood, uncomfortable with Belinda's scrutiny. "I'm going to get some air."

She headed toward the employee entrance. Suddenly, a man stepped out from the shadows and called her name. She turned to him and gasped. "You're not supposed to be back here."

"I know," Desmond said. "But I had to see you."

Anna Marie took a hasty step back.

He held up his hands. "I'm not going to hurt you. I just had to see you."

"You *did* see me and that's all you're going to see." She started to walk past him.

"Please don't be afraid. I don't usually do this. What's your name?"

Anna Marie met his gaze, glad for the veil that concealed her face. "You know what my name is."

"No. What's your real name?"

She stopped a smile and said in a low, seductive voice, "Whatever you want it to be."

"You're a wonderful dancer."

"I know." She began to move around him but he blocked her.

"It's really out of character for me," he said, "but when a man reaches a certain age, he starts thinking that maybe he should try something new."

"That's good," Anna Marie said, a little unsure.

"I'd like to take you to dinner. Or if dinner is too much of a commitment, it could be lunch or coffee. But I'd really like to see you again."

"This is my last night."

"I know. I'm asking you out. Not as a dancer, as yourself."

Anna Marie laughed. "That's impossible. Don't ruin this night by confusing fantasy with reality."

Desmond grabbed her arms and pulled her to him.

Anna Marie stared up at him, alarmed but not afraid. She was used to being accosted by some of their customers, but by now they usually had either offered her a large sum of money for her company or were too drunk to be taken seriously. Desmond was neither and she had to be careful. "Let me go."

"I'll let you go on one condition."

"What?"

"One kiss."

She glanced behind him wondering if she should scream. "No."

"Look, we'll never see each other again. And I want to finish this evening having kissed a beautiful woman who's made me feel more real than I have in a long time."

Her alarm slowly grew into panic. "But you hardly know me."

"Somehow I feel I do." He lowered his voice. "Please."

She should say no and run, but she wasn't going to. One kiss. She'd never see him again and she didn't want to miss this opportunity.

Anna Marie seized his hand. "No one can see us." She led him to a small storage closet and closed the door behind them. She turned to him. "Okay, now—"

His mouth was on hers before she could finish. She didn't remember him removing the veil, she just remembered his warm, wet mouth covering hers, his hands encircling her waist and drawing her close to his hard, solid form. When he pulled away, the only sound was their breathing. He reached and turned on the light.

Anna Marie quickly turned it off and replaced her veil. "Someone might see it and come in."

He turned the light on again. "I don't care. I want to see who I'm kissing."

She turned it off and the moonlight from a small window cast a shadow over his face, leaving his eyes visible. "You said one kiss."

He leaned in close. "I lied."

Anna Marie put out her hand, resting it on his chest, but the gesture was as ineffective as using a feather to hold back a boulder. "Well, I'm going to make you keep your promise."

Desmond rested his hands on the wall behind her and smiled, his teeth glinting in the darkness. "I was afraid of that." His gaze dropped to her veil. "So I can't persuade you for another one?"

Anna Marie swallowed, her voice unsteady. "No."

"You're sure?"

No. "Yes."

He straightened. "Fair enough." He opened the door and motioned that she was free to leave.

Anna Marie wanted to run, but she calmly walked ahead of him.

He grabbed her hand. "Wait a second. I want to give you my number," he said and handed her a folded napkin.

"How classy," she teased.

"I didn't bring any business cards. These are my home and cell numbers. I don't give them out a lot, so that should mean something."

Anna Marie hid a smile. He wasn't original. She was used to getting phone numbers and all of them went into the trash, but she would treasure this one.

She tucked the napkin in her bra. "I'll keep that in mind."

His gaze dropped to her breasts. "You do that."

She lifted his chin then touched his lips with her fingers. "Have a great evening, Desmond," she said then turned away.

He jumped in front of her. "Say my name again."

"Why?"

"Just say it."

"Desmond. Isn't that your name?" she said, looking at the napkin.

"Yes."

"Did I say it wrong somehow?"

He searched her face in wonder. "No, it's just the way you say it reminds me of something. Or someone. I'm not sure." He placed a hand against his forehead. "God, I'm not even drunk. I know I'm not making sense, but there's just something about you that's so familiar." He reached for her veil. "I need to see your face."

Anna Marie stepped back. "I'm sorry, but we have a no-touch policy. The kiss was a favor, but that's all. And now I need to go and don't get in my way."

"What happens if I do?"

She rested her hands on her hips. "Fred warned me about you. He said you were trouble. Do you want me to slap you?"

He stepped closer. "I want you to spend the night with me."

"You're not alone." *Except I'd love to spend the night with you, too.*

Desmond lightly caressed her arm. "You danced for me."

Anna Marie stepped back, each stroke of his fingers making her tremble inside. He threatened to crumble her resolve to resist him. "You're breaking the rules."

"I like breaking rules."

"Somehow I'm not surprised."

"Malika!" Belinda said in the distance. "Do you need me to call security?"

"Give me a minute." She met his gaze. "Do I?"

For a moment he didn't move, his intense gaze making her skin tingle, then he stepped aside and she walked by.

"Call me. I'll give you a week."

She continued walking without looking back. "Or else what?"

"I'll find you."

Chapter 4

"There you are, Rockwell," Julius said when he saw Desmond slip from a backstage exit. "I'd wondered why you'd disappeared." He looked in the direction of the door. "How did you manage that? Their security is tight."

He'd dodged a guard then picked the lock, but Desmond didn't plan on sharing that. "Don't ask."

Julius nodded in sympathy. "You struck out."

Desmond sat on one of the tables. "No, I didn't."

"Did you get a phone number?"

"No."

"Then you struck out, but I don't blame you for trying."

Desmond shook his head. "It wasn't like that. She's different. Someone special."

"Heck, yeah. If she can move like that standing up imagine what she can do in bed."

"I already have."

"And she's tiny, but she has a body on her. I mean her butt alone is worth extra attention. Don't tell me you didn't notice."

Desmond lifted one of the candles. "I noticed that, but I noticed something more."

Julius laughed and slapped him on the shoulder. "My friend, we all noticed it."

Desmond sighed and set the candle down. He knew there was no use trying to explain how he felt. He could hardly understand it himself. Yes, she was sexy and he wanted to do a lot more than kiss her. But he also wanted to get to know her. He wanted to spend time with her and that was rare for him. He didn't even know her and she'd probably danced like that for everyone, but somehow he couldn't shake the sensation that she'd danced just for him.

Julius buttoned his jacket. "Just forget her. You're never going to see her again. Give it up, Rockwell. She's gone."

Desmond glanced at the stage then nodded, resigned. "You're probably right."

Anna Marie sat in an all-night diner trying to come to terms with what had happened. The wig, outfit and makeup were gone so nobody paid attention to the pretty, but unremarkable, young woman in the corner eating a Danish roll and sipping a cup of herbal tea. Somehow, in one night, her life had changed. *She* had changed. She'd kissed Desmond Rockwell—the high-school loner, the delinquent, the boy she'd loved for a year.

He'd kissed her and she'd enjoyed every moment. But she was with Bruno. Desmond was only a dream; Bruno was a reality. Desmond had kissed Malika. What would he think if he saw her now? Anna Marie squeezed her eyes shut. She'd memorized his numbers, but she'd never call him. She had to forget him. It was over. Malika was gone. She was no longer an exotic dancer, but plain old Anna Marie, and she knew he wouldn't be interested in her. Beside, she had Bruno and was happy with her life.

Anna Marie finished her tea, unable to believe the lie. She didn't love Bruno but he was who she had. She was the kind of woman who dated shiftless, lackluster consultants, not men with smiles that could make a woman want to strip naked and say "Take me."

Back in high school, Desmond had barely noticed she was alive. Except for those two weeks, when a harmless crush blossomed into love, but that was a long time ago. She was a grown woman now. Besides, she'd never see him again. She took out her tip, then left the diner and headed for her car. Her cell phone rang as she turned the key in the ignition. She shut the car off and answered the call.

"Where the hell are you?" Bruno asked. "Your book club doesn't usually last this long."

She glanced at her watch. "We had an in-depth discussion."

"You could have called and told me. I've been worried."

Anna Marie sighed, feeling guilty. She knew he cared about her. "I'm sorry. I'm coming home now."

"Great. Hey, babe, could you pick up some beer?"

"Yes."

"Thanks. I love you."

Anna Marie made a noncommittal sound then hung up. She stopped by a liquor store, picked up Bruno's beer and a men's magazine she knew he liked to read, then drove home. He thanked her with a grunt from his favorite position on the couch. Anna Marie went into her bedroom and changed into a pair of pajamas. She then looked under the bed and pulled out her high-school yearbook. It was one of the few items she'd kept. She opened it to a picture of Desmond and ran her fingers over his lips and eyes. He hadn't changed much. Just older and tougher with a hint of devilment in his gaze. Anna Marie glanced up when she heard Bruno's footsteps and quickly shoved the yearbook back in its hiding place.

Bruno entered the bedroom and pulled off his

shirt. "I forgot to tell you before you left. Your sister called. Said she wanted to talk to you."

Anna Marie frowned. She hadn't talked to her sister in three years. It wasn't because of animosity, but lack of interest. Their lives had taken different paths once Child Protective Services had entered the Williamses' home. Anna Marie was ten and Tracie five. They were immediately split up and Tracie was sent to a foster family that eventually adopted her; Anna Marie was never adopted. Tracie had an advanced college degree; Anna Marie only had her high-school diploma.

They'd reconnected when they were in their twenties. Tracie had tracked her down. At that time her sister was a bright twenty-year-old college student with money to spare, while at twenty-five, Anna Marie had already crawled out of skid row twice and had never been on a college campus. Their first conversation had been awkward, but that didn't bother Tracie, who was determined to keep in touch. And they did, mostly through brief phone calls and holiday cards. Sometimes Tracie would pop by when she needed something. Three years ago Tracie had shown up at Anna Marie's apartment in Arlington upset over a broken heart and the thought of her high-school reunion.

Anna Marie had cheered her up and Tracie left happy, then disappeared again. She sent holiday cards, but they didn't speak. Anna Marie didn't worry because Tracie always reappeared when she found Anna Marie useful. "Did she say why?"

"No. Oh, and some lawyer called for you."

"Did he say why?"

"No, just wanted you to call him back." Bruno pulled on his pajama bottoms then got into bed. "Night, babe." He turned, then went to sleep. There was no kiss. Not even a peck on the cheek.

"Good night," she said.

Within seconds he was asleep. She could hear the soft sound of his snoring. Anna Marie sat on the edge of the bed and sighed. Her magical night was officially over.

The following morning, Anna Marie called Tracie and left a message, but didn't get a reply. That didn't worry her; her sister was very clever at doing disappearing acts. She knew if Tracie wanted something really bad, she'd let Anna Marie know.

On Monday, Anna Marie planned to return the lawyer's call first thing from work, but once she reached the office, she discovered that Sandy was in one of her moods and had made Nancy cry. As a result, Nancy couldn't function most of the day and Anna Marie had to cover for her. When she got home that evening, she discovered that Bruno had invited some friends over and had left the living room in a mess before going to meet with one of his "clients." So Anna Marie vacuumed, wiped the crumbs off the coffee table and removed the moisture stains left by the glasses, then made dinner, in case Bruno didn't eat out, before she called the lawyer's office.

"You're lucky you caught me," the lawyer said after Anna Marie introduced herself. "I was just about to leave the office."

"Oh, I'm sorry," Anna Marie said, surprised by how young he sounded. "Perhaps I could call you back tomorrow."

"Why? I'm here now, aren't I? Anyway, my name is Glenn Thornberg. I'm a junior partner here at Thornberg and West and I've been assigned your case."

"My case?"

"Sorry. That came out wrong. The thing is…I have good news for you. You've been left an inheritance."

"What?" Anna Marie said, startled.

"Yes, a considerable property and enough money to keep you comfortable."

"I think you have the wrong person."

"No, it's you. I know it's probably a big surprise. Ms. Williams, you're now a very rich woman. Congratulations. I would like to schedule a meeting with you as soon as possible to get things in order. Would next Wednesday work for you?"

"Yes," she stammered. "Are you sure you have the right person?"

"Yes, we're sure. See you Wednesday."

"Right." Anna Marie hung up the phone then went into the living room. Bruno had returned home and lay on the couch eating his dinner. He hadn't even waited for her. He glanced up when he saw her. "Thanks for dinner."

"I'm leaving you." Anna Marie stopped and covered her mouth. That wasn't what she'd meant to say. She'd meant to tell him about the phone call and that she would rent an office for him so that he could work outside the home and get his business set up properly. But those words didn't leave her mouth.

He continued to focus on the TV. "What?"

She sat down beside him, certain this was the right choice. "Did you hear what I said?"

"You can tell me during the commercial."

Anna Marie raised her voice a bit. "I'm leaving you." This time she did mean it.

"Good. I want to finish this movie. Besides, you need a rest. You've had a long day."

Anna Marie stared at his profile, wondering how she could have been with him for two years, then she got up and stood directly in front of the TV.

He tried to look around her. "Move."

"I will, because—I. Am. Leaving. You.—Enjoy your show." She turned and walked to her bedroom.

Bruno moved his tray out of the way and raced after her. "What are you talking about?"

Anna Marie grabbed her suitcase off the shelf inside her closet and began to pack.

"You can't leave me. You're all I have. What will I do without you?" He spun her around. "You know that I love you, babe."

She yanked herself free and continued to pack. "My name is Anna Marie, not *babe*. And you'll get over me fast."

"No, I won't." Tears filled his eyes. "Why are you doing this to me? I thought we were happy."

"You know we're not. We just don't want to be alone, but it's not working. You need to get a job."

"I have a job."

"A job that can pay the bills. I'm not good for you and one day you'll find the perfect woman for you."

He drew her close. "You're the perfect woman."

Anna Marie pulled away and returned to her packing.

Bruno watched her for a few moments, then said, "I don't believe you're really doing this. I think you're bluffing."

She zipped up her suitcase.

"Oh, I know what this is all about." He held up his hands in surrender. "Okay, you win. I'll marry you. Now do you feel better? We'll get married." He sat on the bed and stared up at her.

She lifted her suitcase and left the room.

He followed. "I don't know what this is all about, but you'll be back and I'll forgive you."

"I'm not coming back." Anna Marie got her coat

out of the hall closet and grabbed her handbag from a hook nearby.

"You're just going to take a suitcase? That's it?"

"That's all I need. The rest is yours." She pulled on her coat, then tossed him a set of keys.

He stared down at them. "You don't know what you're doing."

Anna Marie opened the door. "Yes, I do. I'm starting a new life."

Chapter 5

The next day Anna Marie defeated the Cobra.

"You can't quit!" Sandy said, a vein popping out in her neck as she stared at Anna Marie from across her desk. "You need this job."

"Not anymore."

"You got another job behind my back? Is that what this is all about?"

"No, I don't have another job, but you don't have to worry about me."

"I don't need you anyway," she shouted. "I run this place by myself. Good riddance. Get out."

Anna Marie didn't move from her seat.

Sandy's vein became more prominent. "Didn't you hear me?"

Anna Marie folded her arms. "I have something to say."

"I've heard enough."

Anna Marie nodded, then stood. "I give you ten years."

"What?"

"Before a stroke or heart attack takes you. Goodbye." She left and closed Sandy's door behind her. She'd never have to see her again. Anna Marie patted the doorknob. It felt good to finally say what was on her mind.

Nancy rushed up to her. "Is it true? You're quitting?"

"Yes."

"Where are you going? Does the state have another position open? I'd love to leave here, too."

"I'm sorry, Nancy. There's not another job that I know of. I have an opportunity for something else."

Nancy impulsively hugged her. "Oh, I'll miss you."

Anna Marie awkwardly accepted the hug, not believing her. "You take care of yourself."

Nancy sniffed. "I will."

Anna Marie put her things, which were few, in a small cardboard box, then left. She nearly skipped when she reached the parking lot. The bright spring sun warmed her face and she didn't feel the chill of the breeze that scattered two wayward plastic cups under parked cars. She was free! Free of the Cobra. Free of Bruno. She was starting a whole new life.

But she soon began to doubt the promise of a new life when the lawyer rescheduled twice. Anna Marie stood in her cramped motel room and paced. She'd given the lawyer her new phone number and cell phone. Why hadn't he called?

I'll find you. Desmond's words came to her without warning. It had been almost a week. Would he try to find her? Anna Marie pushed the thoughts from her mind. He'd probably forgotten about her by now. Besides, he couldn't find her. He didn't know who she was. She sat on the bed and stared at the dull orange carpet.

What if it had all been a mistake? Had she left her job and dumped her boyfriend for no reason? She should have waited to get the money first. What if it never came? Would she have to go back begging? She knew Bruno would take her but she could never face Sandy again. Perhaps she should start job-searching.

Friday turned into Saturday then Sunday, then it was Monday again. Anna Marie lay on her bed, staring up at the ceiling as April rain fell outside the window. She didn't mind the rain. It had been raining the day she ended up in a worse-looking motel over sixteen years ago. She'd wondered if she'd made a big mistake then, too. Sometimes she still wondered….

Anna Marie sat up and looked at her suitcase.

She hadn't bothered to unpack because she hadn't planned to stay here, but she knew she had to make a decision. Stay another week or do something. She looked around the motel room and realized the depth of her mistake. She'd been hasty, arrogant. That night with Desmond had blurred her judgment. Bruno cared about her, plain old Anna Marie, when no one else took notice. Bruno wasn't that awful and she'd hurt him. She hated hurting people and now she was alone. But she knew she didn't have to be. She checked out of the motel.

A half hour later she stood in front of her old apartment and raised her hand, ready to knock. This was the right thing to do, she tried to convince herself. Bruno had asked her to marry him so that meant he loved her. Nobody else loved her. She'd find another job and she would encourage him to do the same.

Anna Marie moved her hand to the brass door knocker then stopped. She could hear the TV and men's voices. She imagined Bruno sitting on the couch and how messy the living room would be once his friends left. She let her hand fall to her side. She couldn't go back. Even though her mind said nobody has ever loved you and no one will. She couldn't go back to that life.

"Did you knock?" a voice said from behind her.

Anna Marie turned, surprised to see the pizza delivery guy and glanced down at the order—

calzones. "Um…no. Excuse me." She bent down, picked up her suitcase and left.

Anna Marie drove aimlessly, trying not to focus on her disappointment. She'd had hopes dashed before. Hopes of being adopted. Hopes of having a family of her own. But she didn't care about those things now. She just wanted the freedom that the promise of money could give her. She wanted—no, needed—that to be real. On the right-hand side of the road, Anna Marie saw the local post office. She started to drive past then decided to check her mailbox and made a sharp U-turn. She'd had one for a few years and, just like her night job, Bruno knew nothing about it.

Once she retrieved the items inside, Anna Marie headed over to the wastebasket. She quickly flipped through the stack of bills and junk mail then stopped when she saw an invitation. Who would send her an invitation? She'd never received an invitation in her life. Not to birthday parties, or weddings or baby showers. She opened it and read:

You have been personally selected to join The Black Stockings Society, an elite, members-only club that will change your life and help you find the man of your dreams. Guaranteed.

Anna Marie shook her head and was about to toss it when she noticed something. No other invitations were inside the basket. Usually, people went through their mail right there in the post office and threw away the junk mail, but she didn't see any others like hers. Could it be for real?

The Black Stockings Society? Who were they? Who had sent the invitation? Why hadn't they signed their name? It had to be a trick. Anna Marie waited and watched other people get their mail but no one else had an invitation like hers. She leaned against the counter and looked at it more closely. It was a handwritten note, on expensive parchment paper, lined with finely woven lace in a gold-lined envelope. Perhaps they knew about her inheritance. Maybe they were somehow connected with that. She read on.

Dumped?

No.

Bored?

Yes.

Tired of Being Single?

No.

Ready to live dangerously?

Always.

Then this is the club for you. Guaranteed Results! Submit your application today.

Anna Marie pulled out a pen and smoothed the enclosed questionnaire. She briefly scanned it then folded it up again. The questions were silly.

Would you prefer a motorcycle ride or a trip on a boat? Leather or lace?

This couldn't be real. It didn't make sense. She left the post office, got in her car and started. But the envelope seemed to call to her from the passenger seat. What harm could it do? Answer a few questions, pay the small fee. It could be fun. She turned off her car, pulled out a pen and began completing the application.

Would you prefer a motorcycle ride or a trip on a boat?

Motorcycle.

Leather or lace?

Both.

What would your ideal man be like?

Anna Marie nearly crumpled up the questionnaire. Ideal? There was no such thing as "ideal," especially when it came to men. She tapped her chin as an image came to mind. And yet there was one man who could fit that mold. She thought of the last night she'd danced at The Palace of Sin and hastily scribbled down: Attractive, sexy, rebel and adores me.

She looked at the words then crossed the last ones out. What man like that would adore her? It was impossible. She crossed the rest of the words out, too. Then reread the words *"help you find the man of your dreams. Guaranteed."* Well, if they were going to be that bold, she'd give them a challenge. Anna Marie took a deep breath, then wrote:

I want a man like Desmond Rockwell. Better yet I want Desmond Rockwell. Just for a night I want him to adore me and pamper me and lo—

She stopped and crossed out the last word. She didn't need him to love her. She'd done without love long enough and didn't feel she was missing anything.

Anna Marie looked over her response, satisfied.

Let them try and do that. She read the "sworn oath"
at the bottom of the page:

> *As a member of The Black Stockings Society,*
> *I swear I will not reveal club secrets, I will ac-*
> *cept nothing but the best and I will no longer*
> *settle for less.*

"'I will no longer settle for less,'" Anna Marie
read out loud, surprised by how powerful the simple
statement felt. She looked at her response about
Desmond and hoped they'd be able to read it clearly.
As for keeping her membership a secret, she didn't
have to worry about telling anyone because she had
no one to tell and she was good at keeping secrets.
Before sealing the envelope, she paid the nominal
membership fee by providing her credit card information, then posted it.

But the moment she put the application in the
mail slot, she regretted sending it. She knew what
she had asked for was impossible. And now her
money, although not much, was gone to a society
she'd never heard of and would probably never hear
from again. Anna Marie went back to the motel
and registered for another room.

Two days later, a medium-sized package arrived
for her at the post office. She gave the clerk a yellow
slip to retrieve it then rushed to her car and opened
it—she stared at the contents with amusement. She

held up a pair of black fishnet stockings and grinned. She knew what she could do with them. She set them down, then pulled out three more pairs of stockings and her interest increased. They were excellent quality, expensive and daring, just what she liked. But where would she wear them and with what? Malika would have no problem, but Anna Marie wasn't the type. She quickly placed them back in the box and then looked at the membership card enclosed:

Anna Marie Deena Williams, Member, The Black Stockings Society

And read the instructions:

Welcome to The Black Stockings Society. Your first assignment is to take your membership card to St. Claire's Salon, where you will ask for their Maxi Special. Set aside plenty of time for your first appointment.

Directions with a map and phone numbers were included.

Once you have visited this location, you will select one of your stockings and wear them to your meeting with the lawyer.

How did they know she had a lawyer? Did she still have one? Why did it matter what she wore? Perhaps they wanted her to look more sophisticated. She could do that. But why a secret society? Anna Marie shook her head. Who cared? She was ready to spice up her life. Anna Marie pushed her fear and suspicion aside. She would make this work.

The next day, after a visit to the library, Anna Marie returned to her motel room and was shocked to find shredded paper all over the carpet. She immediately ran out of the room and went down the hall to the manager's office. "I think there's a rat or raccoon or something in my room," she said, trying to catch her breath.

The manager, Arnold Wright, a greasy-looking fellow with a unibrow, barely looked up at her. "Nonsense. We run a top-notch establishment here and I've never had any complaints about rodents. Especially about rats or raccoons!"

"Well, I'm not going to stay in that room until you check it out thoroughly," she said, trying not to sound hysterical, but she hated rodents.

He slowly rose to his feet. "Okay, let's see."

She followed close behind Mr. Wright. When they reached her room, Anna Marie stood at the doorway. She didn't want to risk having some "thing" run over her shoe. The manager looked at the scene, confused.

"Maybe someone broke in."

"Why would someone break in and shred my newspaper?" At that moment, they heard something moving under her bed. Anna Marie jumped on a nearby chair, while Mr. Wright grabbed a small trash bin, ready to crush any critter that emerged. They both stayed perfectly still. Then slowly the creature emerged.

"Oh, it's just a turtle," Mr. Wright said, returning the trash bin.

Anna Marie got down off the chair and walked over to examine it closer. "How did it get in here? Who does it belong to?"

"I don't know, but I do know this—our rules say no pets allowed." He turned to leave.

"So what should I do with it?"

"Whatever."

"What do you mean, *whatever?*"

"Well, *I* don't want it. I know, you can cook it for turtle soup. I hear it tastes good." He chuckled.

"I'm not going to eat it."

"Then throw it in the trash or dump it outside. But you can't keep it here. No pets allowed." He nodded then left.

Anna Marie bent down and picked up the turtle. She could tell from its dark skin, yellowish markings and tall, dome-shaped shell that it was a box turtle.

"So you liked my newspaper, huh?"

In one of her foster homes, a kind foster brother had been fascinated with turtles and taught Anna Marie how to identify the breed and take care of them. The shredded paper was further evidence that her new roommate was a box turtle. They loved to dig and needed lots of dirt, potting soil, shredded newspaper or scraps of carpet to satisfy them.

She didn't care about the motel rules. He, or she, would not be in a stew tonight or any other night. Someone had abandoned him, but she wouldn't.

After securing her newfound friend in a cardboard box, Anna Marie grabbed her coat and headed for the nearest pet store. Luckily she wasn't a beginner and within an hour she had purchased all the necessary items needed to create a home for her little friend. She also stocked up on food. Box turtles ate a wide variety of food such as slugs, worms, crickets, apples, tomatoes, cantaloupe and leafy green vegetables. She knew box turtles loved snails, but she wasn't going to dig up any.

Back home, Anna Marie emptied her shopping bag, fed the turtle, whom she named Nika, then called the lawyer and he told her that he'd be out of town for the next couple days, but that he would definitely talk to her when he returned. Anna Marie didn't want to wait, but didn't know what other option she had. She grabbed a writing pad and wrote down the date he'd return and agreed to call him back then.

After that she called and made her salon appointment. She'd never gone to a salon before and looked forward to the experience.

Anna Marie sat in the luxurious lounge of the St. Claire's Salon eager to get started. She was surprised by how quickly they'd been able to fit her in. The salon was located in an exclusive clothing store on the rooftop level, which provided a breathtaking view while a pianist played classical tunes surrounded by lush plants. Anna Marie sighed with pleasure, ready to enjoy an all-day treatment when her phone rang. She frowned when she saw the number and stepped outside into the corridor to answer it.

"Yes?"

"Thank God, you answered," Nancy said in a tearful voice.

"What?"

"The Cobra is in one of her rages and there's nothing we can do to calm her. You're the only one."

"But I've left that job, remember?" Anna Marie could hear Nancy beginning to cry and softened her voice. "What's the problem?"

"I sent our internal audit report to the wrong department."

Anna Marie sighed in relief. "Nancy, that's not the end of the world. Just call the department head and ask them to return it to you," she said, used to Nancy panicking.

"But that's not the only problem…."

Anna Marie felt a sense of doom. "Then what is?"

"I sent it before it was 'sanitized'!"

"You mean, you…?"

"Yes. Oh God, if the Cobra finds out, I'm dead."

"Where did you send it?"

"I sent it online. I didn't mean for it to go to…"

"You sent it online? Nancy, I told you to always have it either hand-delivered or sent by courier." Anna Marie took a deep breath. "Nancy. Which department did you send it to?"

"Mildred Watson's."

"What!" Of all the divisions that should not see their report prior to it being overhauled was the office of procurement. And Mildred Watson, who was chief executive officer for procurement, had an intense dislike for the Cobra and would be delighted to have something to catch her on. The "sanitization," which was a prerequisite for any of their department's audit reports, meant that they—specifically, Anna Marie, when she was employed with them—skillfully "adjusted" or "added" line items to provide a full accounting for all of the Cobra's expenditures.

Although they were a small office, Sandy traveled a lot. Whether it was to a local, state or national training workshop or conference, they had been told to use phrases such as *per diem, training materials* and *out-of-pocket miscellaneous items* to ensure that all expenses were recorded as business, not personal.

While the Cobra's absence from the office was always cause for celebration, none of them ever challenged her instructions. They did as they were told. Besides, why should they put their jobs in jeopardy when no one from the Management and Accounting Office noticed? Anna Marie had learned quickly not to question where or how monies were spent. She just matched up expenditures with existing grant-funded accounts, making sure both figures equaled each other, got a signature and submitted it.

However, Mrs. Watson was a stickler for procedure and strict when it came to each department's budget. She would spot the inconsistencies. And, if she did, it would definitely result in the Cobra, and everyone else in their division, losing their jobs and possibly facing legal action. Anna Marie knew she had to think fast.

"If they discover what we've been doing, they could eliminate our section," Nancy continued desperately. "We have to look efficient and viable. I need you. Please help us."

Anna Marie glanced at her watch. "But I'm at an appointment."

"Can't you reschedule?" Nancy said with increasing anxiety.

She looked through the glass doors with longing. She was only a few steps from paradise. "Yes, but—"

"Please, Anna Marie, I'm counting on you. We could all lose our jobs because of this. I need this job and Dave is looking for a reason to have complete custody of the kids."

Anna Marie sighed. She recalled the numerous times Nancy would complain about her short-tempered ex-husband. Dave was emotionally abusive and her heart ached to think what the kids would endure if their circumstances changed. "I'll be right there." She reluctantly turned off her cell phone and returned it to her handbag. She went back inside and walked up to the receptionist, a bright-faced young woman with intricately braided hair. "I need to reschedule."

"What's your name, please?"

"Anna Marie Williams."

The receptionist turned to her computer and typed in her name, then frowned. "You're a card member."

"A what?"

The young lady lowered her voice and leaned forward. "A member of the society."

"Yes."

She shook her head. "Then you don't want to do that."

"Do what?"

"Reschedule."

"But I have to and what does being a card member have to do with anything?"

"It has to do with *everything*. I wish I could be a

member. You wouldn't believe the treatment members get here. I suggest you keep your appointment." She returned to her magazine.

Anna Marie tugged on the strap of her handbag. "I can't. It's an emergency."

"Has someone died?"

"No."

"Is someone going to?"

"No."

"Then it's not an emergency." The young lady nodded in the direction of the waiting area. "You'll be seen shortly."

Anna Marie felt her patience thinning. "I can't be seen today because I have to go."

"You're making a big mistake. Rania is *not* going to be happy about this."

"Tell her I'm really sorry, but I'll see her next time."

"If there is a next time," the young woman muttered. She looked at her monitor, typed something then said, "I can schedule you for this Thursday."

"Thank you for your help," Anna Marie said, then hurried out the door.

The receptionist watched her go, then picked up the phone. "Rania, you may have a problem."

Anna Marie was glad Nancy had called when she did. Anna Marie knew people of influence and would use those contacts. She phoned someone who worked in Mrs. Watson's office who had a friend who managed the entire department's computer system and database. This individual was able to intercept and delete the report, before Mrs. Watson saw it.

By early afternoon, everything was done and Anna Marie met Nancy across the street from her old office building. Nancy handed Anna Marie the report then took her to an empty office in another division where Anna Marie could work out of the sight of the Cobra. Anna Marie promptly began working on the report. The due date, when it was supposed to have been sent to the Management and Accounting Office, had passed, and the division chief would be calling the Cobra to find out where it was.

Within minutes, Anna Marie discovered that the problem was worse then she'd expected and she knew she needed at least three days to troubleshoot. She hated having to reschedule her salon appointment again, but knew she had no choice. By the end of the week, everything was in order and she gave Nancy the report, which she had delivered right away. Anna Marie brushed aside Nancy's thanks and offer of a girls' night out. All she wanted to do was go home.

The moment Anna Marie reached her motel she fed Nika, then fell on the bed, ready to fall asleep. Suddenly, someone pounded on her door.

Anna Marie reluctantly dragged herself to the door and glanced through the peephole, but she couldn't see clearly.

"Who is it?"

"A delivery for Anna Marie Williams."

Curious, she opened the door and saw a woman standing there. The woman had a thick braid down her back and wore a fitted suit, looking as though she were a model. However, her expression resembled a drill sergeant. "Are you Anna Marie Williams?"

"Yes."

"My name is Sonia Hernandez and you're in serious trouble."

Chapter 6

Anna Marie stared at the woman, wondering if she should call the police. "Excuse me?"

"I'm with The Black Stockings Society. May I come in?"

Anna Marie opened the door wider. "Sure," she stammered as the woman marched past her and sat on the bed. "Would you like anything to drink?" she asked. "There's a vending machine and—"

"No, I don't need a drink." The woman cast a nervous glance at the shoe box on the floor. "There's something moving in those papers."

"Yes, Nika. My turtle. He likes to bury himself."

"I see."

"How did you find me?"

"It doesn't matter." Sonia crossed her legs. "I'm sure your next question is why am I here?"

Anna Marie leaned against the door. "I am curious."

"You violated an instruction."

"I'm sorry?"

"Sit down."

She didn't want to, but Anna Marie knew an order when she heard one. She sat on the bed near the headboard and faced Sonia. "Yes?"

"In the contract you signed, you promised you would follow the instructions of the society and you did not."

Anna Marie searched her memory, but came up blank. "What are you talking about? I haven't told anyone and—"

"You cancelled your appointment at the salon."

"Oh, that. I told the receptionist I had an emergency."

"Twice?"

"The emergency was bigger than I expected."

Sonia opened her handbag and pulled out Anna Marie's signed contract. "If you look carefully at the small print on the back, it specifies that you are obligated to follow the rules. You are allowed one missed appointment but two are grounds for automatic dismissal."

Anna Marie read the information with dread,

then looked at Sonia with dismay. "So I'm out before I'm even in?"

Sonia folded the contract and replaced it in her handbag. "We discussed your case and decided to give you some leniency."

"What does that mean?"

"You're on probation."

"Probation?"

"Just for a few weeks until you get a handle on things. We have to do this for some of our 'special' inductees. You need to know how the society works. Members know their worth. They don't put people ahead of themselves at their own expense. There's a distinct difference between being helpful and being a dishrag. I've been assigned as your trainer. Most people jump right into the society but others, like you, need trainers like me, so I'll stay with you for a couple of days until you're ready to go out on your own."

"But I am ready," Anna Marie protested, terrified of the thought of having this woman or anyone staying in her life. "I love the stockings and I promise I will follow the instructions from now on."

"It's too late."

"It's just that something came up and—"

"Do you want to be a part of this society?"

"Yes."

"Then you're stuck with me." The woman stood and walked around the room. "First off, what are you doing here?"

"I left my old apartment. I made a big mistake because I thought I was moving into this new house I had been told I'd inherited and that I was going to live on the money, too, but the lawyer canceled and—"

"Did you reschedule with the lawyer?"

"Yes, but he had to travel and he told me to call when he got back. I thought I'd wait a day or so because I don't want to be a bother."

"So you'd rather stay in this dinky little motel when you could be in a house?"

Anna Marie glanced around the room. "Well, when you put it like that, of course not."

"Then what are you going to do about it?"

"I don't know what you mean."

"You need to call the law office and tell them that you want an appointment as soon as possible. You can give them a specific date and if they cancel, let them know that you want someone else assigned to your case."

"Can I do that?"

"It's your money, isn't it?"

"Yes, at least I think so. I'm—"

"Yes or no?"

Anna Marie took a deep breath. "Yes."

"Then do it." Sonia handed her the phone.

She stared at it. "You want me to call them now?"

Sonia shoved it in her hand. "Why wait for tomorrow?"

"What if he's busy?"

"He'll make time for you."

"But—"

"You know what's wrong with you?" Sonia continued before Anna Marie could reply. "You're a rich woman who's acting poor. You have to demand what you want."

Anna Marie frowned. "I'm not rich yet and I don't know how much I'm inheriting so—"

"You're going to be rich someday so you might as well act the part now. Make demands."

Anna Marie didn't believe her and she didn't like the word *demand*. It made her think of Sandy and one nasty foster father who forced her to clean out his shed every other day. She didn't want to be like that. "I don't want to upset anyone."

"You're not going to upset him or her by letting them know what you want. Now dial and tell them you want an appointment as soon as possible. No buts."

"There's one thing."

Sonia reached over and took her hand. "Stop pretending. I know who you are."

Anna Marie froze. "What do you mean?"

"Do I need to show you the pictures?"

Sonia knew she was Malika? "You have pictures? Are you blackmailing me?"

Sonia sighed. "No. I'm just trying to let you know that we at the society know that Malika and Anna

Marie are one and the same. If you don't believe me then let's pretend just for now that you're Malika. How would she handle this?"

"She would—"

Sonia shook her head and nodded to the phone. "Don't tell me, show me."

Anna Marie took a deep breath, then dialed. When the lawyer answered she deepened her voice and gripped the phone. "I need to schedule a meeting with you as soon as possible. If you can't, I want to work with someone else in your firm. If that's not possible, I will take my story about your incompetence to the papers and tell them that I've had to wait a ridiculous amount of time just to speak with you about my inheritance. Do I make myself clear?" She glanced at Sonia, who silently applauded.

"Yes," his voice cracked. "I'm sorry I—"

"I don't need your apology, I just need a date."

"Thursday at two?"

"See you then." Anna Marie hung up, then stared at Sonia, feeling numb.

"What time did he say?"

"Thursday at two. I've never been Malika in the daytime."

"Fun, isn't it?"

Anna Marie grinned. "Wonderful."

"You're a fast learner. If you want a new life, then you have to act a new way. First you're going back to the salon."

"I have to make an appointment."

"I've already made an appointment for you. You're going to see them tomorrow then you're going to get some new clothes. Then you'll be all set for the lawyer. Now let's move."

"Move?"

"Yes. I'm not staying in this place. After I've selected a hotel, we'll get something to eat."

Two hours later, the two women sat in an expensive restaurant booth designated for members only. Anna Marie studied Sonia. "So how did you get involved with this society?"

"I was recruited."

"Recruited?"

"Yes, there are different levels in the society. There are associates and members, then recruits or trainers like me."

"How were you recruited?"

"I can't tell you."

"Well, how was I nominated?"

"I can't tell you that, either."

"Why not?"

"Because you don't need to know. Only three people know exactly how the society works. One is the founder, Ms. Dorathe, and two other individuals who are senior members and only go by initials."

"Why all the secrecy?"

"Why not?"

"But how did you find out about me?"

"You were nominated. Your nomination went through a strict screening process. You were observed."

"Followed?"

"Observed," Sonia firmly corrected. "Deemed suitable and selected."

"And then I failed."

"Yes. You failed yourself. Fortunately, failure isn't permanent and I'm here to help."

"What do you get out of this? Wouldn't you rather be a member than a recruit?"

Sonia pulled out her cell phone and showed Anna Marie an image on the screen. "That's my family."

Anna Marie gasped at the picture of a man and two small children in front of a magnificent house. "You're rich."

"In more ways than one." She pointed to the man. "That's my husband and my children, Hilary and Douglas."

"Wow," Anna Marie said, not knowing what else to say. She knew that pictures lied, that smiling faces didn't always mean a happy home, but from the look on Sonia's face, she could sense a feeling of pride and love for the people in the picture. Anna Marie felt a stab of envy then brushed it aside. "When you have all this, why are you a trainer?"

"I love my job. I love working with people like you. I like seeing your dreams come true. Mine already have. We recruits are a special force. Associates help you, but we trainers make things happen. And I'm going to make sure that a lot of good things happen for you."

Early the next morning, Anna Marie sat in St. Claire's Salon ready for her appointment when her cell phone rang. She looked at the number, then Sonia. "It's Nancy."

"She can leave a message."

"But it could be urgent."

"You no longer work there, remember?"

"But—"

She held her hand out. "Give me your phone."

Anna Marie reluctantly handed it to her.

"Hello? Yes, you have the right number. I'm Anna Marie's secretary and she's busy at the moment, but if you leave a message she'll get right back to you… No, she can't speak to you right now. Nancy, I know you're a smart woman and if you take the time to think, rather than to panic, you will be able to solve your problem. If you can't, I suggest you start looking for another position you can manage. Goodbye." Sonia hung up. "She didn't want to leave a message."

"Did she tell you what the problem was?"

"She can handle it." Sonia tucked the phone away.

"You're going to keep it?"

"You have better things to do." She gestured to a waiting attendant.

Whoever said it was impossible to have heaven here on earth had not been to St. Claire's Salon. At first, Anna Marie felt awkward, not used to having anyone touch her entire body, much less a team of four. The day spa, which was called An Affair to Remember, was located inside the salon, and was definitely very expensive. In the entryway was a softly flowing waterfall, elegant leather lounge chairs with small TVs and headsets to occupy clients while they waited. Anna Marie had been sitting for only a few minutes before the woman at the reception desk informed her that Rebecca would be out shortly.

Within minutes a tall, willowy young woman in a black kimono came out and led her to a changing area.

"Hello, my name is Rebecca. I'm going to be the one in charge of your facial today. You will need to change into this robe and slippers, so that you will be comfortable during your stay with us." She then opened a drawer and handed Anna Marie a freshly washed spa robe and pair of lush slippers. "Just push the button when you're ready."

For the next hour Anna Marie found herself being covered with expensive face creams and delicious-smelling lotions; however, this was only after Rebecca had assaulted her face with several mechanized tools and instructed her to take better care of her skin. The next attendant, a woman with porcelain features, led Anna Marie into a dimly lit treatment room. "I am going to give you a full-body massage I know you will enjoy," she said.

She was right. Anna Marie's body and mind gave in to Stephanie's gentle manipulation of her body. She surrendered to the tactile pleasure, aromatic smells and soothing music and fell asleep.

The third attendant, an aggressive-looking man with an eyebrow ring, took full control of Anna Marie's unruly mane. He trimmed and cut Anna Marie's hair, giving it incredible shape and then applied a permanent soft-wave curl. The final effect was amazing. "This curl will last up to three months," he told her. "And when you have it done again, you can either make the curls bigger or smaller, and I can mix and match the size of the curlers to give you any style."

Anna Marie's last appointment was with a makeup artist. She hadn't expected to learn much. As Malika, she had no problem utilizing makeup to accentuate and sexualize her good features. As Anna Marie, however, she'd never taken the time to see what makeup could do and used a minimal amount when going to work.

The makeup artist, a very attractive woman in her mid-forties was an expert with over twenty-five years in the profession. She showed Anna Marie how to add instant sparkle to her eyes and make it look like it was natural by using a dark brown eye pencil to outline the corners of her eyes. She also instructed Anna Marie to use dark brown mascara, instead of black, for her lashes, again making them look natural.

Lastly, she showed her the proper use of foundation and powder, then helped Anna Marie fill in her eyebrows, which were nearly nonexistent. From a distance or up close, the result was dramatic, but natural-looking, and gave Anna Marie instant confidence.

When Sonia saw her, she grinned. "Your lawyer is going to pay a lot of attention to you. And your schedule is clear. While you were in there, I canceled all your other appointments."

"All of them?"

"Yes. *No* is such a wonderful word."

Following the salon makeover, they settled into the Claremont Hotel, one of the most expensive in the city. When Anna Marie began to protest Sonia told her that all expenses were covered by her membership. Three days later, Sonia took her shopping. Anna Marie looked forward to the adventure. Growing up, she had worn secondhand clothes, and while she had dressed appropriately for work, unlike when she was Malika, Anna Marie didn't have the kind of wardrobe she desired.

"We have appointments with a personal shopper in three of the finest stores in town," Sonia told her as she drove to their destination. "You are going to be very busy today."

"Okay," Anna Marie said, unsure what a personal shopper did. She soon found out. In each store, a personal shopper took her measurements, looked her over, asked her a few questions and then went out on the floor, selected and brought back items to her dressing room they felt suited her. If something didn't fit, or needed to be in a different color, they went looking—all she had to do was stay in the dressing room and try them on.

By the time they got back to the hotel that evening, both of them were exhausted and hungry, but Anna Marie found herself unable to eat. She was so excited about all the things she had bought that day, she decided to try on several select pieces again before going out to dinner.

The day of her appointment with the lawyer, Anna Marie stared at her image in the mirror. She wasn't sultry Malika. But she wasn't plain old Anna Marie, either. Sonia had helped her select what to wear and they both decided on a formfitting, square-necked, empire-waisted cream linen dress, a three-quarter-sleeve cashmere cardigan and a provocative pair of two-inch black satin pumps. And of course, her first pair of stockings—thigh-high black fishnets. She was someone new and she liked what she saw and she was ready for a performance....

Sonia looked at her with joy. "My work here is done."

"You mean you're leaving?"

"You're ready to handle the rest on your own. Good luck."

"Thanks. I'll need it."

She hadn't called him.

Desmond hit the tennis ball with extra force. Finding her had proven to be harder than he'd thought. It was like she was a ghost. He had to forget her. He wanted to, but he couldn't.

He finished his volleying then headed for the locker room and showered. He'd just changed when his cell phone rang.

"You've got to help me, Rockwell," his colleague Glenn said. "If I cancel again, she'll kill me."

"Who?"

"The Williams woman. We're the trustees of her estate, but I overbooked. I know you don't usually do this kind of stuff, but—"

"I hate doing that. You know I only work with Advent."

"I know and I'll make this up to you. Please. It's real simple." Thornberg briefly gave him the logistics. "I've left the folder in your office on your desk. It should be easy."

"When is your appointment?"

"This afternoon."

"When?"

"At two."

Desmond glanced at his watch and swore. "It's 1:45 p.m."

"You can make it. I know how you drive. Thanks, Rockwell." He hung up.

Desmond swore again then threw his things into his bag. He wished someone would fire Glenn, but knew they wouldn't. He was a nephew of one of the partners. Everyone knew that Desmond's job was working directly with Advent, and keeping abreast of his real-estate holdings, businesses and other investments was enough. He'd paid his dues handling wills, estate holdings and other trivial things like that. One more stunt like this and he didn't care who the kid was related to.

He swore. This was supposed to be his day off. All he had were a pair of jeans and a sweatshirt. He could stop by his home to change his clothes, but he didn't have enough time. He hated keeping clients waiting. Desmond sighed, hoping this client wasn't a pain.

Chapter 7

Anna Marie sat in the waiting room, amazed by its ostentatious setting. She never knew civil attorneys could make this kind of money. She picked up a glossy women's magazine and started to read an article when the front door suddenly opened and a man burst through and headed for the receptionist. Anna Marie instantly recognized him and leaped to her feet. She watched him bend over the front desk.

The receptionist, an older woman with her hair pulled back in a crooked bun, stared at him, surprised. "What are you doing here?"

"Cleaning up one of Glenn's messes, what do you think?"

"Well—"

"When Anna Marie Williams arrives, please send her to my office."

"She's already here." The woman gestured behind him to Anna Marie, who stood paralyzed in place.

He turned and looked at her. He hadn't noticed her before, but he certainly did now. His manner was professional, although his initial gaze at her dress and legs hadn't been. He walked over to her and held out his hand. "I'm Desmond Rockwell. I'll be handling your case today. Sorry," he said when he caught her looking at his jeans. "I know I look like I make a poor replacement, but I was called in at the last minute. You can rest assured that I'm good at what I do."

"I can believe that," Anna Marie said in a choked voice, her heart racing.

He narrowed his gaze. "Have we met before? I feel as though I know you from someplace."

Behind him the receptionist snickered and he groaned, then playfully said, "Be quiet," before he turned back to Anna Marie. "I know that sounded like a really bad come-on. I didn't mean it like that." He turned. "Anyway, please follow me." He held open a heavy glass door.

She'd follow him, jump him, strip him or whatever he wanted. Anna Marie couldn't believe her luck. She begged her legs to keep her upright and thankfully fell into a chair once she reached his office. He closed the door then smiled at her. She swallowed. He looked even better in daylight—he had gorgeous dark brown eyes and she already knew what his soft lips felt like on hers.

She had to focus. His intense first look had been dangerous. She couldn't let him connect her to that night.

Desmond sat on the edge of the desk and folded his arms. "So where do I know you from?" He adjusted and balanced his weight. Anna Marie tried not to stare at how his jeans revealed his well-defined thighs.

"Why are you sure that you know me?"

"Because I never forget a pretty woman and somehow your name means something to me. I also get the feeling that you know me."

"Why?"

"When I shook your hand, you looked at me as though you'd seen a ghost." He folded his arms. "Refresh my memory."

Anna Marie licked her lips. "We have met. A long time ago."

"How long?"

"Very long."

He leaned forward. "Now I'm intrigued. Why are you so hesitant to tell me when and where we met?"

Anna Marie crossed her legs, pleased that he noticed the movement. "It may change your opinion of me."

"You don't know my opinion. Right now, you're a mystery. Come on, tell me. I have an interesting history. Did we meet in juvie or something?"

Anna Marie lowered her gaze and her voice. "Or something." She raised her gaze. "Remember Hallon House?"

Desmond jumped away from her as if she'd grown spikes. She knew he didn't want to remember the halfway house and the two weeks of hell he'd spent there. *She* certainly didn't, but couldn't help it. Nearly sixteen years ago, it had changed everything for her....

"What do you think you're doing?" the security guard said, standing next to her.

"Just looking," Anna Marie said, determined to make her voice sound casual, although the nightdress she'd stuffed under her coat had made a small bulge. She hoped he didn't notice.

"I think you're doing more than that. Come with me."

The moment he reached for her arm, she ran.

"Stop her!"

Another security guard blocked her path but she managed to dodge him and escape out of the store. She ran through the mall, easily darting through the crowd of people. She couldn't get caught. If her foster mother found out, she'd get rid of her for sure and she didn't want that. Mrs. Bell provided her the best foster home she'd ever had. She just had to get rid of the evidence before they caught up with her. She ran around a corner and crashed into a solid form.

She glanced up and saw Desmond Rockwell, who at seventeen already had a reputation in their school for causing trouble and breaking hearts.

"What's the rush?"

"Let me go. They're after me."

"Who?"

"The guards."

He unzipped her jacket and pulled out the night-dress and panties. "Man, who taught you how to steal? You never want your jacket to bulge like this. We've got to get rid of this." He glanced around then tossed the two items behind a vending machine. He turned to her, then stopped. A second later she knew why.

"Don't move," the guard said, breathless.

Another athletically built guard appeared and smiled. "Rockwell. I should have known she'd be one of yours."

"I'm not one of his," Anna Marie said, not wanting him to get into trouble.

The athletic guard looked at her with pity. "Of course you'd lie for him. You think he's worth it. He's not. He's got three others like you."

"I'm not lying. He's—"

"Turn around and put your hands up against the wall."

Anna Marie got into position and they searched her. "She's clean."

"Doesn't matter, we've got her on tape."

The guard patted Desmond down then laughed with triumph when he pulled out a small plastic bag. "What's this, Rockwell?"

Desmond grinned. "Herbs from my grandmother's garden."

"Your granny grows marijuana?"

"Don't know what you're talking about, sir."

"Trying to bring some of your family's island habits to the States?"

"Herbs are good for you."

"What would your father say?" He didn't give Desmond a chance to reply, instead he pulled out his handcuffs and nodded to the other officer. "Cuff her."

They were led outside the mall and into separate squad cars. The next thing Anna Marie knew, she was standing before Judge Gilamore, a man known to be sympathetic to young offenders. He believed in rehabilitation rather than punishment so he sentenced her to Hallon House. There were whispers that Hallon House, a residential treatment program, was a welcome alternative to being sent to a juvenile detention center. But Anna Marie wasn't sure.

Unfortunately, she didn't have a choice and soon found herself on the residential campus located on 2.5 acres plus a 150-acre working ranch for special projects and activities, located twenty-five minutes west of Charlottesville, Virginia.

Structure and discipline were the main focus and her days were filled with intensive therapy, academics, fitness and nutrition training, life skills and self-introspection.

Anna Marie remembered her first encounter with the grounds and building. It wasn't as austere as she'd imagined and provided a focused environment where she learned responsibility, work ethic, self-esteem and appropriate social and life skills. Unlike many of her foster-care placements, where she was the "new kid," other teens joined on a continual basis. Oddly enough, it was the only place Anna Marie felt safe.

Privileges were earned for jobs performed well, appropriate behavior and signs of improvement of any life skill. Initially, getting used to the strict duties was extremely difficult for Anna Marie. The daily routine consisted of waking up at five in the morning, light calisthenics, breakfast—and breakfast chores, such as setting the table, cleaning up and washing dishes—and fieldwork assignments. All residents were assigned to either feeding the chickens and cleaning out their coops; herding and, when needed, shaving the sheep; feeding the pigs; tending a large vegetable garden or cleaning out the horse stalls.

Anna Marie was a model resident and earned many privileges because she was a hard worker and learned fast. She used her privileges to roam the grounds. She'd been there for three days when she found Desmond in the stables.

Anna Marie stood for a moment, stunned as she watched him cleaning a stall. She'd never experienced sexual attraction until she let her eyes gaze upon Desmond's tight jeans and bare back as he spread the hay. Her palms grew sweaty and her stomach tightened, but she didn't move. "You're here?"

He spun around then smiled. He wiped the back of his hand against his forehead. "You were worried about me?"

She nodded. "I didn't mean to get you into trouble."

He shrugged. "Trouble follows me. I know how to take care of myself. Besides, I've been sent here three times before. The judge thinks I have potential. I'm not sure what he sees, but I'm grateful."

Anna Marie nodded then stared at his tattoo.

He noticed her looking and came closer so she could get a better look. "Like it?"

She nodded again.

"I've got another one, but I can't show you where it is right now."

Anna Marie felt her face grow hot.

"Where do you go to school?"

She told him and he nodded. "Same here."

Yes, she already knew that. She didn't bother to tell him that they had the same homeroom because it wouldn't matter. "Thanks for talking to

Mrs. Bell for me. I mean sending her that letter. She told me about it. What you did really meant a lot to me."

He shrugged, embarrassed. "Yea, well, you're a good kid." He leaned against the rake. "Why did you do it?"

"Some girls at school said I could join their group if I stole some items."

"Not Shana and gang?"

"How did you know?"

Desmond shook his head. "I just know. Look, for a guy she's a great la—" He stopped. "Never mind. Stay away from her. You don't want to get messed up with her."

"Okay."

He flashed a slow smile, which was more mature than his age. "You don't want to get messed up with me, either." His smile grew. "But you don't care about that, do you?"

She shook her head.

He leaned forward and tweaked her nose. "You're lucky you're not my type. Or you'd be in serious trouble."

She already was in trouble. Anna Marie had never loved anyone before, but that day, that touch changed everything. She didn't know why and she didn't care. She remembered the first day she'd seen him in school. She was a new student and he was the boy with a reputation. At that time she didn't know what his reputation was, but she admired his aloof manner and handsome looks. Once she'd given him a pencil and he'd smiled at her as if she'd given him something a lot more personal. She'd blushed, although by that time she knew what his reputation was.

He never returned her pencil, but she never asked for it back. Today he'd taken her heart and she wouldn't ask for it back, either. She knew she loved him and nothing would change that. "Why did *you* do it?"

"My herbs?" he said with a note of sarcasm.

She nodded.

"I didn't plan on getting caught."

"You're a smart guy, you could do anything. Why do you do what you do?"

Desmond glanced away. "Because it's what people expect, but one day I'm going to—" He looked at her and shook his head. "Never mind."

"Tell me."

He paused. "Promise not to tell anyone?"

She crossed her heart. "I promise."

"One day I'm going to be rich. I don't know how, but that's what I'll do."

"I believe you."

He grinned. "You probably still believe in the tooth fairy."

Anna Marie shook her head, her gaze serious. "No, but I do believe you can do anything."

Desmond met her gaze for a long moment then lowered his head, uncomfortable, and cleared his throat. "I'd better get back to work."

"I can help you," she said. "I'm fast and strong."

"You have the time?" he said, amazed.

"Yes, I have lots of privileges."

"Like what?"

"I can roam, get books from the library, choose my dessert."

His face brightened. "You can get ice cream? I'd rather have that than another cupcake."

"We could switch at dinner."

"You're on."

"So can I help you? I have nothing else to do."

Desmond motioned to another rake, then winked. "Then get to work."

For the next week and a half, Anna Marie became Desmond's shadow. Luckily, their monitor didn't seem to mind. They ate together—he ate ice cream every day—worked together—he told her he'd like to get a Swiss Army knife one day because it had everything—but at night they went to different dorms, where Anna Marie dreamed about him. Anna Marie didn't want their sentence to end, but it did the moment a silver Mercedes drove up and a young woman in her late teens got out and saw Desmond. She kissed him and he spun her around while Anna Marie watched them, hot tears burning her eyes. She turned and marched back to the stables. She rested against the stable doors and watched one of the horses eat.

"There you are."

She stiffened at the sound of his voice and blinked her tears away. She was good at that. So when she turned to look at him, there was no sign of her sorrow.

He walked toward her. "Who's coming to pick you up?"

She shrugged. "I'll take a taxi."

"What about Mrs. Bell?"

She shrugged again. She hadn't wanted to bother her.

"Let me take you home."

"I'm all right, really."

He leaned against the stable door and looked down at her. "You owe me."

"What?"

"I don't want to be left alone on a two-hour drive with that girl. Dana thinks there's more between us than there is and it suits me because she has an influential father, but right now things could get sticky."

"But you kissed her."

He raised a sly brow. "You saw that?"

"Yes."

"I kiss a lot of girls."

Except me.

He took her hand. "Please let us take you home."

"Okay."

"Good, we'll wait for you."

Minutes later Anna Marie emerged with her suit-case, prepared to face Dana's annoyance. But the moment the girl saw her, she smiled. "Let's get out of this place."

Anna Marie crawled into the backseat. Desmond sat beside her.

"What are you doing?" she whispered. "You're supposed to be up front with her."

"Why? Is this seat reserved?"

Dana spoke up. "Is there a problem, you two?"

He rested his arm around Anna Marie's shoulders and covered her mouth with his hand. "No."

Dana started the car and Desmond let his hand fall. As they drove his hand slipped down to the front of her blouse.

Anna Marie turned to him and said in a quiet voice, "You said you like trouble?"

"No, I said Trouble follows me."

"How about pain?"

"I don't like pain."

"Then I suggest you remove your hand."

"Give me a break. In only a few months I'll be eighteen then I'll really get into trouble messing with girls like you."

"Not if you behave yourself."

"I find that difficult."

"I can teach you." She pinched him hard.

He yanked his arm away. "Lesson learned," he

said, then closed his eyes and fell asleep. As they rode he leaned against her then slowly his head rested in her lap. Anna Marie didn't know if she should push him off or let him sleep. She looked to Dana for help, but she kept her gaze focused on the road. So Anna Marie let him sleep, pleased to have him near her. When they reached her house, Anna Marie had to wake him. For a moment he looked up at her, surprised, then his smile returned. "Stay out of trouble," he said.

Anna Marie nodded and got out. Dana handed Anna Marie her suitcase. "I know that sounds ironic coming from my cousin, but he means it."

"Your cousin?" Anna Marie stared at Desmond, who stood on the other side of the car grinning.

Dana looked at him. "What story did you tell her?"

"I don't know what you mean," he said.

Anna Marie pointed at him. "You lied."

"How else was I going to get you to come with me?" He saluted then disappeared inside the car.

Dana sighed wearily. "Talk about a black sheep. Take care of yourself."

Anna Marie nodded then watched them drive away.

Back at school, Anna Marie ducked every time she saw him and he was never without a girl at his side. Now, years later, she couldn't hide. She didn't want to.

Chapter 8

Desmond took her hands and lifted her to her feet. "I don't believe it," he said, measuring her with his eyes. "Anna Marie Williams all grown up. You still look like you can get a man in trouble."

"No, you were the only one." She folded her arms. "Does that make a difference?"

"You mean the fact that you're the reason I spent two weeks in HH? No."

"You've done well for yourself." She sat down, her hand burning from his touch. "No longer getting into trouble."

He laughed. "That's only a matter of opinion. It's nice to see you again. What are you doing here?"

"My inheritance."

Desmond blinked. "Oh, right. Yes, now I re-member." He went behind his desk and sat. He opened a folder then handed her a legal-sized envelope. "Let's start with this."

Anna Marie looked at the worn item tied up with a blue ribbon. She knew of only one person who used to do that. Before she touched it, she knew who it was from. The pain of the loss hit her. She'd always imagined Mrs. Bell alive but the envelope told her she was dead. Anna Marie took it, undid the ribbon and carefully opened it.

My dear little Anna Marie,

If you are reading this letter, you already know that you are now the sole heir of every-thing I possess. I am both happy to do this, but sad that I couldn't be there to see you one more time. I failed you years ago and hope that I can make that up to you now. I trust you as I've never trusted anyone and I've always considered you to be my daughter.

Yours with love,

Mrs. B

Anna Marie let the letter fall to her lap, too stunned to do anything but sit there. She hadn't cried in years and she wouldn't start now, although regret threatened to consume her. If only she'd gone

back just once to explain. Mrs. Bell had died thinking she'd failed, when Anna Marie knew she'd
failed her.

"What did she leave me?" Anna Marie asked in
a wooden voice.

"Quite a bit of property and financial investments. You'll be a rich woman after you complete
the conditions."

She folded the letter and replaced it in the envelope. "Conditions?"

He frowned. "I'd hoped she'd put this information in the letter."

She put the envelope in her handbag. "No."

Desmond quickly glanced at the folder Glenn
had left and scanned what was inside. "You have to
stay in her boarding house for six months."

"She has a boarding house? I didn't know they
still existed."

"Most don't, but that's what she called her
place." He read on. "There are three boarders
living in the house at present and it's up to you
whether you'll renew their leases after six months
are up, and the time you take ownership. Until
then you'll get a monthly allowance of three thousand dollars."

"After six months what happens?"

"You'll get a million dollars."

Anna Marie's mouth went dry. "You can't be
serious."

"I am. It's all here. Looks like Mrs. Bell was a clever woman."

"Why would she leave that much to me? And why would I have to stay in her house? What kind of people live in a boarding house anyway? Usually transients and day workers, right?"

"To be honest, I don't know. From what I see here in her folder and what she's left you, I doubt she'd make you live with criminals. I'm sure you'll manage. The question is what will your husband think?"

"I don't have a husband."

"How about a boyfriend?"

Anna Marie smiled, understanding the significance of his questions. "No. You?"

"No, I don't have a boyfriend."

"You know what I mean."

"Yes, and you already know the answer to that." He read further. "Oh, by the way, you have until tomorrow to make a decision."

"Tomorrow! That's not enough time for me to think this over."

"You can thank Glenn's delay for that. Mrs. Bell stipulated that you had a certain number of weeks after her death to decide, but because of Glenn, you don't." He rested his arms on the desk. "I say go for it. Six months isn't that long."

Anna Marie stood, unsure. "I guess."

He put her file away. "Do you have any plans for tonight?"

"No."

"Good. Let me take you to an early dinner. We'll come back for your car later," he said, coming from around his desk. "I just need to change my clothes. My condo isn't far from here. And I promise I won't try anything."

"That's disappointing," she teased.

He grinned and opened the door. "Don't worry, Anna Marie, I don't disappoint."

He was right. When Anna Marie stepped into his living room, she could hardly believe what she saw. The room was bigger than two hotel suites combined. It had a modern feel with an eclectic collection of one-of-a-kind designer furniture making the area look sleek and sparse. She couldn't miss the enormous Ultrasuede loveseat facing the large picture window with a breathtaking view and the "sunken" area that curved around the open fireplace, which was in the middle of the room, with its plush beige carpeting.

On one side of the fireplace was a minibar and on the other was an enormous theater-style flatscreen television. She could only imagine what the rest of his condo looked like, but she didn't have time before he emerged from his bedroom wearing a suit. "This place is amazing," she said in awe. "You did it all."

"Surprised?"

Anna Marie shook her head then sat down on an ottoman. "No, I knew you would."

He folded his arms and studied her. "You always did. Why?"

Because I loved you. Anna Marie shrugged and made her voice casual. "I guess, like the judge, I knew you had potential."

Desmond grinned. "You were the only two people who did."

"And we were right." She bit her lip. "I assume you got all this legally?"

His grin grew. "Well, I'm not selling 'herbs' anymore. Yes, everything is aboveboard. The only time I'm in the courtroom is to represent someone else."

Anna Marie surveyed the room again. "You must be proud of all this."

A shadow crossed his face, but quickly passed. "Sure. Now let me really impress you."

Moments later they sat in an exclusive French restaurant with a skyline view of the city. Desmond lost little time getting acquainted; instead he fell into his role to impress her with the knowledge and ease of a man used to the best things in life. Anna Marie felt uncomfortable and asked him to order for her. He ordered a bottle of champagne then treated her to smothered shoulder of lamb, cabbage-and-potato cake and a pear-and-rose-hip tart for dessert, along with his favorite ice cream.

"I barely saw you after we left HH," Desmond said.

"You were hardly in school," Anna Marie said, hoping to divert him from the real reason. "I can't believe you graduated."

"They wanted to get rid of me, but don't change the subject. What happened to you?"

Anna Marie looked around. "This place is amazing."

"Why do I get the feeling that you don't like to talk about yourself?"

"Because you're really smart."

"Too bad, because I'm interested." He rested his chin in his hand. "Start talking."

Anna Marie reluctantly set her utensils down. "There's not much to say. I certainly haven't become a rich lawyer with a great apartment."

"I know. That's *my* story. Now what's yours? What happened after you left HH?"

"I went back to school and graduated."

"And then…?" he urged.

"I ran away."

"Why? I thought you liked your foster mother."

"I did. She was wonderful. I—I didn't want to be a burden to her so I thought it was best that I leave. I worked odd jobs before I got a great government position and I worked in different departments until I got the call about the inheritance. See? Nothing interesting."

Desmond shook his head. "Somehow I don't believe you. You look like a woman with fascinating secrets."

"Well, that's the only story you're going to get."

"For now."

They ate and talked about old times, then had dessert—raspberry ice cream.

"What do you think?" he asked.

"It's delicious."

"Thanks, it's one of my favorites."

"I remember you loved ice cream."

"Still do. Especially when it afforded me all this."

"Really?"

"Yes, my ex-wife and I started a nice little brand of our own called TraDesmo Ice, a line of gourmet flavors, then we sold it to a big company for several million."

"Millions? You're a millionaire? And you were married? Who was she?"

"Actually, I'm a multimillionaire, but we don't need to get specific. And yes, I was married, but it doesn't matter who she was. It's over."

"Why are you working as a lawyer? You don't need to work at all."

"No, but I have to have something to do. I have one client who keeps me busy and I have my own schedule that suits me."

"But you don't sound as if you enjoy it."

He shrugged. "It's what I do. I have no complaints."

"Oh." Anna Marie suddenly fell silent, not knowing what else to say. He was even more than she'd imagined. Far from the Desmond she'd known or dreamed about. A businessman, a lawyer? At one time their lives had been similar, now they were worlds apart. He'd done so much with his life. He'd fulfilled his potential. She hadn't. Who had his ex-wife been? A sophisticated CEO? A model?

"What's wrong?" Desmond asked, sensing her altered mood.

She plastered on a smile. "Nothing. I'm really happy for you."

"I haven't changed, if that's what you're thinking."

"I wouldn't blame you if you had."

"I haven't and I can prove it." He stood. "Let's go have some fun."

The loud beat of the dance club released Anna Marie's inhibition. The bodies, the heavy bass beat, the flickering lights liberated her. She moved, entranced. Music always made her lose herself. She felt Desmond's body next to her. He moved well to a seamless rhythm that was sensual and intoxicating. It was a moment before she felt him slow down. She looked up at him and he stared down at her with a peculiar expression. "What's wrong?" she asked.

"Nothing. You can really dance."

Anna Marie flashed a bright smile. She had to remember to control herself. She couldn't let him remember her as Malika. "I'm thirsty." She headed for the bar and placed an order.

Desmond sat beside her, still staring at her in a strange way. "I'm sorry about that," she said. "I didn't mean to embarrass you. I can get carried away."

"You didn't embarrass me. Come on, let's go."

"But my drink…"

"I'll get you another drink somewhere else." They exited the club and Anna Marie headed for his car, then noticed he was walking in another direction.

"I thought we were going back."

"Not yet."

She turned around and followed him. They walked down the main street. Cars raced past while the club music became a distant rumble in the spring evening. Soon they arrived at another club, The Thrill, which had more subdued music with a slower rhythm. Once on the dance floor, Desmond pulled her into his arms and started to sway to the music. "Who are you, Anna Marie?"

"I don't know what you mean."

"I want to know your secrets."

"I don't have any."

"I don't believe you. When I saw you in my office I was blown away, but when I saw you on that dance floor I wasn't sure who I was seeing. It's like you were a totally different woman."

Anna Marie caressed his face, determined to distract him. "It's your imagination."

"Maybe." He kissed her, his mouth demanding a response she readily gave him. It was even better than she remembered. He drew away and stared at her with that same intensity she recalled that night at The Palace of Sin. She couldn't have him discover the truth.

She spun away. "I really have to go. It's late and I have to move tomorrow."

Desmond followed behind silently, then said, "When can I see you again?"

"I'll call you."

"I don't believe you."

She stopped and looked at him, surprised. "Why not?"

"Rockwell!" someone called.

Desmond turned and Anna Marie sighed with relief that she was free of his scrutiny. She turned and saw Julius waving from across the street. He checked the traffic then jogged over to them. "I've been trying to reach you on your phone."

"What's the trouble?"

"No trouble. Just thought you'd want to have another night of fun." He looked at Anna Marie. "But I see I'm already too late."

"This is Anna Marie Williams. Anna Marie, this is Julius Advent."

She'd seen him so many times before she felt she already knew him. "Nice to meet you."

"Same." He turned to Desmond. "Just came from The Palace of Sin. They have a new dancer. She's good, but not as good as Malika."

Anna Marie tugged on her handbag strap. "If you two want to chat, I'll just wait in the car."

"No, that's all right. I'm heading your way, too." Julius sighed. "Ah, Malika was the best."

"Who's Malika?" Anna Marie asked slyly.

"An exotic dancer. Every man who saw her fell in love with her, including poor Rockwell," Julius offered.

"Shut up, Advent," Desmond retorted.

"He couldn't help it," Julius said. "I—"

Desmond sent him a venomous look and Julius stopped. He tugged on his jacket sleeve. "I'll see you later."

"Good idea."

He waved goodbye then left.

Anna Marie sighed, trying to make her comment casual. "I guess when it comes to a fantasy woman and a real woman, men prefer the fantasy."

Desmond took her hand and looked into her eyes. "No, real men prefer the real thing. I know I do."

And yet you wanted Malika that night. It was a nice statement but she didn't believe him. "I really have to go home."

"All right."

They didn't talk on the way back to his office, where Anna Marie had left her car. Desmond parked then walked Anna Marie to her Volkswagen.

"Did I convince you?" he said.

She put the key in her car door. "You're better than I remember."

He stopped her from opening the door. "When can I see you again?"

"I don't know. My schedule is very busy."

He touched the side of her face and lowered his voice. "What are you afraid of?"

The fact that I still love you. "I have a feeling you're still close friends with Trouble."

He grinned. "Not as much." He opened her car door, his gaze intense. "I'll give you a couple days to call me. If you don't, I know where you live."

Anna Marie sat inside her car and looked up at him. "And you'll come get me?"

He closed the car door then winked. "That's a promise."

Chapter 9

"I bet you the first thing that woman is going to do is throw us all out so that she can get high-paying clientele."

Leona Mathew looked over at Gerald Delaney, a large man in his late sixties with small features and bushy sideburns, as he sat in his favorite chair. She then turned to the other resident, Jane Dye, a paper-thin woman in her sixties with lovely features, who wore a shabby, reddish-brown wig. She sat in the corner playing a Brain Age game. "Mrs. Bell said she'd take care of us after she died."

"Not much the dead can do when they're gone," Leona said.

"They can haunt places," Jane said, still focused on her game.

"This place isn't haunted," Leona said. "Besides, Mrs. Bell was too good a woman not to be resting in peace. I'm sure she's a nice young woman," she said, trying to ignore her apprehension. Why had Mrs. Bell left the house to a stranger they'd never heard of? She'd taken care of the house for these past eleven years. Hadn't that meant anything? Leona pushed her bitterness aside. Mrs. Bell had been good to her, letting her live there in exchange for cooking and doing some housecleaning. This was her home—this was their house. Now, once their leases were up, they would have to leave and they had nowhere else to go.

"We'll see," Gerald said. "Did you see how many trunks the movers brought? Expensive looking, too."

Leona nodded. She'd been the one who had to instruct the movers where to put the trunks. "Yes, I saw them."

"I got a glance at what was in one of them," Jane said with a giggle. "I was wondering what was taking the movers so long and I spotted them putting the items away. There were lots of expensive clothes and shoes."

Gerald's frown increased. "A rich city girl. She'll probably take one look at this property and see what it's really worth and sell it."

"We have our leases," Leona reminded him.

"Which end in six months."

Jane set her game aside. "I wonder if Mrs. Bell told this woman anything about us."

"She would have to."

"No. I mean the truth."

They were silent with fear, then Leona said, "Mrs. Bell would never have revealed that to a stranger. She was good at keeping secrets."

Gerald grunted. "We all know the moment this woman finds out the truth, she'll get rid of us in an instant."

"So, it's agreed," Leona said. "We make sure she doesn't find out anything."

All three of them turned to the window when they heard a car approaching. They watched Anna Marie walk up the pathway then stop.

"Why is she stopping?" Leona wondered.

"Looks like she's remembering something," Jane said. "It's like she's lived here before."

"Hmm," Gerald said. "I wonder how she knew Mrs. Bell. She's too young to have known her the way we did."

"Maybe," Jane said. "She's pretty."

Leona frowned. "And dangerous. Remember, she's not one of us, but be pleasant," Leona said as she headed for the door. She was used to Jane's and Gerald's ways but didn't want them to do anything to upset the new owner. She wiped her sweaty palms on her jeans then opened the door. "Hi, you must be Ms. Williams."

"Anna Marie, please," Anna Marie said, stepping inside.

She was smaller than Leona had expected, with a low, melodious voice. "Can I help you with your bags?"

"This is it." She nodded to her shoebox. "Plus Nika, my turtle."

Leona stared at the single suitcase and the shoebox, surprised, then remembered. "Oh, yes that's right. You had most of your things sent ahead."

"Right."

"I'm Leona. I live on the lower level."

"Nice to meet you."

"There are two other tenants who would like to meet you." She turned and led Anna Marie into the living room, quickly grabbing her duster and hiding it behind her back. She'd spent all day cleaning, but hadn't dusted the items in the far end of the living room yet. "This is Gerald and Jane." The two residents stood and shook Anna Marie's hand before sitting again.

"A pleasure," Anna Marie said.

Jane offered a tentative smile. "Yes."

Gerald grunted.

Leona sent him a look then said, "Let me give you a quick tour."

Anna Marie didn't need one, but didn't say anything. She allowed Leona to show her the kitchen and dining room. They had been altered a little, as had the living room. The chairs looked a little more worn, but were just as sturdy and the table was still a gleaming mahogany where many large dinners had been held. Before going upstairs, Leona showed Anna Marie the hall closet, then opened the door to the basement.

"I don't need to see the basement," Anna Marie said. Leona sent her a strange glance, but Anna Marie didn't care. She wasn't going down there. Ever.

"Okay, let me show you the rooms upstairs." She pointed to Gerald's and Jane's rooms then led her toward the back of the house and said, "Here is your room. We hope you like it."

Anna Marie walked into the room, not sure she believed Leona's reassuring words. She wondered what Leona was doing here. She was an able-bodied woman in her forties with a great figure and a nice face. Why was she staying in a boarding house with two people who were much older? Didn't she have any family?

Anna Marie set her suitcase down, placed the shoebox on the bed and then lifted the cover. She could sense they didn't want her here and she wasn't sure she wanted to be there, either. The moment she saw the two-story house, Anna Marie couldn't believe how little had changed—the sloping roof, the third front step that creaked and the green shutters that should have been painted blue to match the trim. When she stepped inside she'd expected the sound of children and the scent of freshly baked cookies, which Mrs. Bell let the younger children help her bake. She was fostering four children with her at that time, but kids from the neighborhood frequently came to visit.

Inside hadn't changed as much as the residents. They were far from young and looked at her with wariness. A wariness she understood. When she'd first arrived, the other kids had looked at her with the same expression. The same suspicious looks, and displays of jealously guarded territory.

Anna Marie smiled at Leona. She could sense her nervousness and resentment that her forced pleasantry couldn't hide. And there were silent questions in the older woman's gaze that she couldn't answer. No, I don't know why she left the house to me. No, I don't know why I have to stay here for six months. But I want the money so I will be living here whether you think I deserve to or not.

"This room has a great view. Mrs. Bell always loved it and it's very quiet. You don't have to worry about the others. I hope you'll like it here."

She'd said that before and Anna Marie still didn't believe her. "I'm sure I will."

"Not much goes on here, but it's a nice little town and the people are friendly."

"I know. I used to live here." The room was like an old friend with few changes.

"Mrs. Bell didn't tell us about you."

"I was one of her foster kids."

"She stopped doing that years ago. One of the kids ran away and she never recovered from that."

"She shouldn't have stopped," Anna Marie said with regret, sadness tightening her heart. "She was a good mother."

"Did you keep in touch with her?"

"No, and I don't feel guilty. She was better off without me."

"And yet she still—" Leona stopped but Anna Marie silently finished the sentence. *Left the house to you.* Leona took a step back. "I'd better go get dinner."

"You cook for everyone?"

"Yes, and clean. I take care of things. We eat together in the dining room. We're like a family."

"I see." Anna Marie knew she wasn't one of them. Once again she didn't belong. She was an outsider.

Leona walked toward the door, then stopped. "We'd hate for anything or anyone to break us up."

"I doubt anything will."

Once Leona left, Anna Marie unpacked, then wandered around the room, finding a perfect spot for Nika. She opened the closet, surprised to see the amount of clothes there. Sonia had taken care of having all her purchases delivered. She'd never owned so many things. Anna Marie freshened up for dinner, determined to make a good impression. Years ago she'd only had two pairs of jeans and one pair of shoes that squeaked when she walked. Now she was a professional woman not as easily intimidated. Six months and then the money was all hers. The money was all that mattered.

She heard lively conversation as she walked downstairs. It stopped the moment she entered the dining room. She smiled and sat in an empty chair beside Jane and began making her plate. "Smells delicious. I'm sure it tastes even better."

Leona looked at the others. "Thanks."

Twice Anna Marie tried to restart their conversation, but they only gave her curt replies. Finally Gerald stood. "There's a game on I want to finish." He took his plate and left. Jane soon followed, saying the air in the dining room felt stuffy. Then Leona said she needed to go clean the kitchen. Within minutes the table was empty and Anna Marie sat alone.

Anna Marie finished her meal despite the tightening of her throat, the heaviness in her chest and the threat of tears as she faced the weighty echo of their cold rejection. She remained at the table, looking out the window as the sunlight moved across the room as the sun set, until it completely disappeared.

As time floated by, Anna Marie allowed her memory to flood her mind with the cruel taunts and teasing she'd faced going from home to home and school to school. She remembered the days she pretended she didn't care, when she did. She'd loved it here, but she never felt safe. She was always afraid that Mrs. Bell would send her away. But tonight the rejection hurt more and she didn't want to be alone. She ran up the stairs, raced to her room and then grabbed her cell phone. She dialed without thinking, only realizing who she'd called when she heard Desmond's voice.

"Please, I need you."

"Anna Marie?"

"Yes, please come. I don't want to be alone tonight."

"Are you sure?"

"Do you want me to change my mind?"

"I'll be right there."

Anna Marie sat waiting for Desmond on the porch, a lonely figure in white. She stood as he drove his car up the driveway and his headlights created a silhouette of her form underneath her nightdress. His body responded with a feeling of lust, but he managed to dampen it as he shut off the car engine. Desmond casually walked toward her, instead of running and grabbing her the way he wanted to. He could read nothing in her gaze, which made him uneasy about why she'd called him. He knew from experience that women could be changeable so he had learned to act with caution. He stopped a few feet away from her and hooked his thumb in his belt loop. "What's—"

She moved closer to him and pressed a finger to his lips. He would have been fine if she hadn't touched him, but that simple motion sealed her fate. He no longer cared about the reason why she'd called him; his hunger for her could not be ignored. He pulled her to him and bent to kiss her. She met him halfway, and her willing mouth only fueled the fire within him. His hands encircled her, finding the satin shield of her nightdress a cruel barrier to what he really wanted—the feel of her skin against his fingers.

Anna Marie suddenly drew away and said in a breathless rush, "Not here." She began to turn, but Desmond wanted her close to him. He lifted her up in his arms. "Just show me the way."

"Upstairs, second door on the left."

Desmond made his way up the stairs, but stopped when she gently bit the sensitive part of his earlobe. "If you don't stop that, I'll drop you."

"I'm encouraging you to move faster."

He continued up the stairs. "I'm going as fast as I can." He stopped at the top and looked around. "Which door is it?"

She pointed and he walked toward a brown door then said, "Open it."

Anna Marie hesitated. "There's just one thing."

"I'm not interested."

"But—"

"I'll open it." He draped her over his shoulder, ignoring Anna Marie's gasp of surprise, then opened the door. He turned on the lights, then stopped. The room looked like a bordello. "What the hell?"

"I wanted to warn you," she said, poking him in the back. "Mrs. Bell had interesting tastes."

Desmond gently placed her on the bed. "I like it." He pulled off her nightdress and to his delight she wasn't wearing anything underneath. He stared at her full breasts and his gaze went down from there. "But I didn't come here to look at the room."

Anna Marie pressed her body against him. "That's good to know."

Desmond removed his clothes with such violent intensity, some of the buttons on his shirt scattered onto the wooden floor, but he didn't care. He drew her tender, ripe body to his, determined to claim her soft, smooth body as his own and she was equally determined to claim him. There were no gentle moans of pleasure or tender gestures of desire. Their passion was wild, exhilarating and dangerous.

They had no inhibitions between them, unaware of how vulnerable they'd become to each other. Their raw desire was almost tangible as they sought pleasure in each other's arms. As he filled her with his hunger, she welcomed it without question. It was an exquisite indulgence he didn't want to end.

Anna Marie didn't want it to end, either. She surrendered to him with sweet abandon. She needed this. In his arms she didn't feel discarded, undesirable, unwanted or alone. She needed to be touched; she needed to have him explore every part of her body without limitation, as though she belonged to him, because tonight she did. Completely.

With every move of her body, Anna Marie wanted him to know it—to feel it, to sense it. To sense that when he touched her breasts, her thighs and the sacred place in between, she was his.

Finally, they stopped from exhaustion and lay in bed languid with ecstasy, unable to move.

"Do you have to go?" she asked him, tracing a circle on his back.

He didn't move. His voice was a deep rumble when he spoke. "Do you want me to stay?"

"Yes. I don't want to be alone tonight. Especially in this house."

He turned to her. "You're not alone. There are other people here."

"Yes, but they hate me, just like the kids did before."

Desmond lifted himself onto his elbow and drew down the sheet so he could see her breasts. "I'm sure they don't hate you." He kissed each nipple.

Anna Marie laughed. "Not everyone feels about me the way you do."

He playfully narrowed his eyes, then said in a low growl, "They'd better not." Suddenly, his gaze grew serious. "I thought you had fond memories of this place."

"I have fond memories of Mrs. Bell. Anyway, I now have Nika."

"Who?"

"My turtle. He likes to stay in his shoebox and hide. Anytime I let him out, he disappears under the bed or a dresser. I'd introduce you, but he's shy around strangers."

The corner of Desmond's mouth quirked in a smile, but he didn't laugh. "I'll give him time."

"Thank you." Anna Marie drew up the covers. "I can't make you stay, but if you have to leave, please wait until I'm asleep."

"Are you sleepy?"

"No."

He drew the cover down again. "Good, because I don't plan to leave anytime soon."

Anna Marie woke up alone. She wasn't surprised. Her dream had come true. She'd wanted one night with Desmond Rockwell and she'd gotten it—she hadn't expected to wake up with him beside her. She knew that dreams could never withstand the glare of day.

She glanced at her clock, then heard a buzzing noise. It took her moment to realize it was her cell phone. She searched in her handbag and answered "Hello?"

"Did I wake you?" Desmond asked.

Anna Marie sunk back into her bed, her knees weak from the joy of hearing his voice. "No, I was up."

"Sorry I couldn't stay. I have some business I have to take care of. But if you need me tonight, I don't have any plans."

Anna Marie fell back on the bed and grinned. "I'm glad to hear that, Mr. Rockwell, because I *will* need you."

"I'm always happy to be of service."

She rolled on her stomach and put her feet in the air. "In fact, I may need you the rest of the week. Solving these cases of loneliness takes time."

"Yes, and I wouldn't want you to be lonely," he said in a husky whisper.

"I miss you already."

"What are you wearing?"

"Nothing. Just a big smile."

He groaned. "I'm not sure you're good for me." He laughed. "And I don't care. I'll see you tonight." He hung up.

Anna Marie dropped her cell phone on the bed and screamed into the pillows. She'd slept with Desmond Rockwell and he was coming back tonight! It was more than she could have ever hoped for.

"You're getting cantaloupe today," she told Nika.

She was in high spirits as she prepared for the day and decided to select something fun to wear from her closet. She selected a two-piece white-and-blue-striped sleeveless pantsuit and white leather pumps, then bounded down the stairs. However, the cold reception she received effectively dampened her spirits.

Again she ate alone. Whenever she entered one of the "common areas," like the kitchen, dining or family room, the conversation either stopped or the boarders got up and left. Her questions were met with terse replies or, sometimes, no reply at all. It continued this way for the next several weeks. Anna Marie endured their coldness because her nights were so pleasurable. Being with Desmond healed every slight and hurt she suffered during the day. And she thought everything was perfect until Sonia showed up.

Chapter 10

"What have I done now?" Anna Marie asked, letting her shoulders slump.

"We won't discuss that out here. Let's go to your room." Once inside Anna Marie's bedroom, Sonia closed the door and pointed to a chair. "Sit down."

She did. "What—"

"You haven't called Rania," Sonia said with the same drill-sergeant expression she'd had before.

"Oh, that," Anna Marie said with a dismissive wave of her hand. "I remember reading instructions to call Rania at my earliest convenience. I've been busy. I've met with the lawyer and moved in here and…" she faltered.

"And what?" Sonia pressed. "You don't work, so what has been keeping you busy?"

Hiding in her room had been her main priority. "I've been getting used to everything."

"You've been delaying. You don't want to do it."

Anna Marie squirmed in her chair. "I just don't think it's necessary. To be perfectly honest, I'm not sure I need this society anymore. I'm really not a group person and besides, my life has already changed. My dream has already come true. I spent one night with Desmond Rockwell. Actually, more than one night, and everything is perfect."

Sonia frowned, unimpressed. "Perfect?"

"Yes."

"Then why is it that you didn't introduce me to any of the residents here?"

"You wanted to meet in my room."

"That's not an excuse."

"And also because the society is a secret and—"

"You could have introduced me as a friend. Don't pretend you haven't lied before. You rushed me to your room as though that's the only place where you feel comfortable. Why is that?"

"The boarders and I don't get on. They don't want me to be here. I don't blame them so I stay out of their way and they stay out of mine."

"And you call that *perfect?*"

"Okay," Anna Marie admitted in defeat. "It's not, but—"

"And about Desmond. Wouldn't you also like to be with him in the day?"

"It's not like that," Anna Marie said, annoyed.

"Because you're not giving the relationship a chance. Wouldn't you like to wake up beside him and then spend the whole day with him?"

"I didn't ask for that."

"But isn't that what you want?" Sonia shook her head. "You're settling for less, Anna Marie, and that's against the oath. You're going to make your appointment with Rania right now."

Anna Marie stifled a groan. "But the instructions said she wants to show me home decoration. Why would I need to know that? Homes are for families and I never plan to have one."

"Even though you want one?"

Anna Marie crossed her arms but didn't reply.

"You're doing everyone a disservice. Why do you help the wrong people, like Nancy, Bruno and Sandy, and hurt the ones who need you, like the boarders and Desmond?"

"I haven't hurt anyone," Anna Marie said, stunned by the accusation.

"You're a wonderful woman hiding yourself in this room. With Desmond you only give one side of you. He deserves a complete woman. A woman who can be there day *and* night. A woman he can trust round the clock. And those residents downstairs need someone like you. Mrs. Bell was a smart woman. She knew that when she was gone, you would be what this place needed. Anna Marie, you have a generous heart, but you're afraid to share. Yes, it's been broken, but it can be healed."

Sonia sat on the bed. "Now you're going to do three things. Tomorrow you will go to Rania. Then you'll wear your second pair of stockings on a date with Desmond."

Anna Marie shook her head. "He's not going to ask me out."

"Yes, he will and you'll say yes. And number three, you'll share a meal with the residents. I don't care how, just make it happen."

"But—"

"What's the oath?"

Anna Marie reluctantly repeated it and Sonia smiled. "Good. I'll check on you next month."

Anna Marie fought to stay awake as she followed Rania around the large furniture store. She found the striking, full-figured, dark-skinned woman fascinating but everything else held little interest. She didn't belong here, she thought as she watched a couple walk past. Her gaze fell on the young families and older ones; the pairs who looked like newlyweds and the ones who looked as if they'd been married for years.

She vaguely listened to Rania's commentary and pretended to be interested. She didn't see any point in knowing about color choice or the right fabric or choosing the right couch, but her membership required she get this chore over with. Finally, Rania decided to break for lunch.

"You hate this, don't you?" Rania said, looking at Anna Marie over their turkey salads.

Anna Marie blinked. She didn't want to upset her. She seemed very nice. "No, I don't hate it."

"A home reflects the people who live in it."

"Yes, but I'm more an apartment type of girl."

"Anywhere can be a home. It's all about creating a place of peace. A sanctuary."

"Of course," Anna Marie said, unconvinced, but she was willing to say anything to maintain her relationship with Desmond. She didn't want this dream to end yet and she'd do whatever the society wanted her to do so that wouldn't happen.

"When we go back to the store, I want you to select five items that will turn the boarding house into a home."

Anna Marie didn't know what she meant but was willing to do anything to make Rania happy so they could leave.

After they finished eating, they returned to the store. Anna Marie wandered for several minutes before making her selections. She chose an ovesize leather recliner, an adjustable remote-control floor reading lamp, a hexagonal glass dining table with matching burgundy upholstered chairs, a handcrafted computer cabinet with a rollout desk and file cabinet and lastly, several colorful, large throw cushions. When the items were delivered that weekend, Anna Marie placed them in appropriate locations throughout the house.

Nobody said anything, but she caught Jane's quick smile. That Saturday evening she went into the kitchen, where Gerald and Jane sat at a small table while Leona cooked. She saw a stack of dishes and utensils for the table.

"Let me help you," she said and picked up the plates.

Leona took them from her. "I usually set the table and I don't need any help."

Anna Marie wasn't sure what it was, Jane's frown or Gerald's smile, but something in her snapped. She snatched the plates back. "That's fine, but I'm going to help you so you better get used to it." She looked at Gerald and Jane. "I will set the table and you will eat with me. I don't care if you don't talk to me because I've dealt with worse. I've been spit on, punched, gone a week without food, been locked in a closet and felt a buckle against my back more times than I can count. So you can ignore me and shun me all you want, but that's not going to defeat me because I'm not going anywhere."

They stared at her, but didn't argue.

"You have so much," she continued. "You have a family. Something I've never had and if it is so hard for you to be nice to me, then I truly feel sorry for you. I don't know why Mrs. Bell left me this house and maybe I don't deserve it, but I'm going to honor her wish because I hurt her years ago and I want to make up for it any way I can." She paused and took a deep breath. "And don't worry. I have no plans to get between you and this house. In six months I'll sign it over. I don't want it. And I'll be gone and you can have your family back. I won't miss you and you won't miss me, but I'm here now, so deal with it." Anna Marie marched out of the kitchen, into the dining room and set the table for four.

The first few minutes of dinner started with an awkward silence, then Jane said, "My father was a bastard, too."

"I didn't know mine," Gerald said.

"I haven't seen mine in years," Anna Marie said.

"We're sorry," Leona said. "We haven't been nice to you and this is your house."

Jane bobbed her head in agreement. "Thanks for the new pillows. They really brighten up the living room."

"I think the place needs more changes," Anna Marie said.

"Yes," Gerald said. "The railing could be sturdier."

"And perhaps we could get new carpet in the family, I mean, TV room?" Jane said.

"And some updated kitchen utensils would be nice," Leona added.

Anna Marie nodded. "After dinner, let's write down everything we want and what needs to be worked on or fixed and start from there."

"It could get expensive," Gerald said.

"That's okay," Anna Marie said. "I have money."

They finished dinner then Jane followed Anna Marie into the living room. Jane continued to give suggestions while Anna Marie sat with a pad and wrote them down.

"That's my chair," Gerald said to her.

"Is it? I'm surprised because it's the worst one in the room. It's too soft and is terrible for someone with a bad back. You need something sturdier, like that lovely one near the window under the lamp." She gestured to the new recliner. "But if you want to claim this second-rate one, that's fine by me." Anna Marie began to stand.

He frowned. "Wait. There's no reason to move if you don't have to." He sat in the other chair, then nodded. For the rest of the evening, the ladies continued their discussion on needed changes.

"We've thought of every place but the basement," Gerald said.

"I'm sure it's fine," Anna Marie said quickly.

"Sure, we'll deal with it later."

Leona sent her a look. "What do you have against the basement? It was Mrs. Bell's favorite place in the house."

Anna Marie doodled in the margin of her notepad. "I know."

Jane's gaze darted between the two women, then she said, "Let's think of what we can do to the outside."

Over the next few weeks as spring turned into summer, everyone worked on painting, waxing, nailing and fixing up the boarding house. In the morning they discussed what they planned to accomplish that day and at night they played board games, watched TV and at times just read and enjoyed each other's company. Anna Marie introduced them to Nika and showed them how to take care of him. Gerald played with him and told Anna Marie stories of his youth. Jane showed Anna Marie her Brain Age game and Anna Marie helped her select a better fitting wig and showed her how to do different hair styles. She helped Leona try new recipes and they both had fun learning to use a new food processor and bread machine. Everyone helped around the house. When Sonia stopped by to see Anna Marie's progress, she was amazed.

However, despite her busy schedule, Anna Marie still devoted her late-night activities to Desmond and thoroughly enjoyed them. They went dancing, drinking, to the movies and clubs. She didn't want to change anything. The night suited her. It was enough.

Then he changed the rules.

* * *

"Are you free next Saturday?" Desmond asked her one day over the phone as she sewed a button back on one of Gerald's shirts.

"Sure."

"Good. I'll pick you up after breakfast."

Anna Marie stabbed herself with the needle then winced and swore. "You mean Saturday *morning?*"

"Yes, I want to take you somewhere."

She sucked on her finger, then shook it. "In the daytime?"

"Yes, are you busy?"

"No. Um…okay, how about you come over for breakfast?" She didn't expect him to say yes and nearly dropped the phone when he did.

"Great. See you then."

"Yes." She hung up, then ran downstairs. "Leona, I think I made a mistake. I just invited the guy I've been seeing to breakfast."

"That's okay. There'll be plenty."

Gerald said, "About time you introduced us to your boyfriend."

"He's just a guy I'm seeing, not my boyfriend."

"From the sounds coming from your bedroom, he's seeing an awful lot of you."

"Gerald!" Leona said.

"It's true. I know about sex."

"Why are you worried?" Jane asked.

"It's just…I don't know."

"Don't worry, we'll be on our best behavior."

Anna Marie wanted to believe them but still couldn't stop thinking that the invitation was a mistake. She tried relaxing with a book when her cell phone rang. She looked down and saw her sister's number.

"At last," Tracie said with an edge of annoyance. "Where have you been?"

Anna Marie set her book aside, knowing that any kind of relaxation was now impossible. "I left a message."

"Bruno told me you left him."

"I did. What's wrong?" Anna Marie asked, determined to change the subject.

"Nothing. I've missed you and want to see you. It's been a long time. Where are you staying?"

"I don't think—"

"I'll bring lunch. It will be fun! Please," she begged.

Anna Marie rolled her eyes to the ceiling. "Fine."

"Great. I'll see you tomorrow."

Anna Marie gave her the address and directions, then hung up.

"Who was that?" Jane asked.

Leona frowned. "Don't be nosy."

Anna Marie sighed. "It's okay. That was my sister, Tracie."

"I didn't know you had family," Jane said. "You don't look happy to hear from her."

"I love her because I'm supposed to, but I don't like her very much."

"I have a sister like that," Jane added.

"Well, mine is coming by tomorrow for lunch. If you want to disappear, I won't blame you."

"Is she anything like you?" Gerald asked.

"She's nothing like me."

He grinned. "Then this I have to see."

Anna Marie knew that the others would be interested in Tracie's visit, but she could do without seeing her. First she had to find something to wear. Her sister always made her feel like a "don't." Not that Tracie could help being naturally tall, with flawless features and brownish-black hair that fell in natural waves around her face. But that fact didn't make Anna Marie feel any better about her visit. She needed courage. Then a thought came to her. She opened her drawer and pulled out another pair of shimmery extra-sheer stockings and smiled.

Chapter 11

"How quaint," Tracie said, staring up at the small A-frame house.

Anna Marie ignored her sister's condescending tone. "It's comfortable."

"And you live here with other, um…?" she searched for a word.

"Boarders? Yes."

"What do they do?"

"They don't work. They're retired." I think.

"What did they used to do?"

"I don't know."

"You mean you're living with people you don't know anything about? Do you think that's wise?"

"They're harmless."

"I still think you should check. You probably don't have enough money to afford to do a background check, so I'll do it for you." She followed Anna Marie inside and stopped. "Why is there a spiderweb in that corner? You need a housekeeper."

"I have someone who does the cleaning."

"Then fire her and get someone who knows how to do it right."

"Keep your voice down. They're in the next room." Anna Marie walked into the living room. "This is my sister, Tracie."

Each of them introduced themselves and Tracie smiled, then excused herself to use the restroom. When she reemerged Anna Marie showed her the dining room. Tracie placed the picnic basket she'd brought with her on the table, casting a glance at the living room. "I will definitely find out what's going on here," she said as she took several items out of the basket.

"What do you mean?"

"First, that woman with that horrible-looking wig seems shifty and that old man seems very suspicious."

"You're just prejudiced because this is a boarding house."

"I care about you. You're my big sister, but you don't take care of yourself the way you should."

"You look great," Anna Marie said, determined to change the subject.

"Thank you."

Anna Marie waited for a compliment about her new look, but it never came. She didn't care because she knew she looked great and had decided to wear the same outfit when she met with Desmond.

"Why did you leave Bruno?"

"Because our relationship wasn't working. What's going on with you?"

"I just—"

"Stop pretending, Tracie. You never think of me for no reason."

Suddenly, her sister fell into the chair and her eyes welled with tears. "You hate me, don't you?"

"I don't hate you."

"I know I've made some mistakes. One was not getting in touch with you sooner."

"I'm fine."

"And my divorce has left me very shaken."

Anna Marie handed her a napkin. "Your divorce? I didn't even know you'd been married."

"It was a rush job. We weren't married that long. Two years. I loved him and I lost him and now I want him back." She wiped her eyes with the napkin. "But I know getting Desmond back won't be that easy."

Anna Marie nearly laughed at the coincidence. How funny. They'd both been involved with a man with the same name. She unwrapped a sandwich and took a bite. "His name is Desmond?"

"Yes, Desmond Rockwell."

Anna Marie nearly choked.

Tracie didn't notice. "He's a lawyer, but he doesn't have to be. I thought once we sold the business he'd relax, but he was still so restless."

Her sister had married her one true love? What were the odds? Out of all the men in the world, she'd married him? She wanted to scream.

The doorbell rang.

Anna Marie jumped to her feet and said, "I'll get it," and reached the door before anyone else could. She opened it and saw Desmond. She stared at him as though he'd appeared out of thin air. He stared at her with the same expression of surprise then a naughty grin touched his mouth.

"Somehow you knew I was coming."

She blinked, unable to focus. "What?"

"And you wanted to make me happy." His gaze swept her body. "You look fantastic. Especially the legs."

"Thank you," she said, gripping the door.

He pulled her close and kissed her. "I thought I'd surprise you and take you to lunch."

She shoved him away and sent a cautious glance behind her. "This isn't a good idea."

He looked at her, confused. "Why?"

"I have a visitor."

"Then I'll introduce myself." He started to walk past her.

"No, you don't want to do that."

"Why not?"

Tracie came around the corner. "Anna Marie, your food will get cold." She halted. "Desmond?"

He froze. "What are you doing here?"

She walked toward him. "Visiting my sister."

He glanced down at Anna Marie as though he didn't know who she was. "Your *sister?* I didn't even know you had a sister. I thought you were an only child."

"With my adopted family, yes. But—well it's complicated. What are you doing here?" she asked, with a predatory look in her eyes.

"I came to see Anna Marie."

"Why?"

"Because I'm seeing her—"

"About some things," Anna Marie interrupted. "I'm his client. I acquired this house through an inheritance and Desmond, I mean, Mr. Rockwell, is helping me with the logistics." She looked at Desmond, begging him to play along.

Tracie turned to him. "I thought you didn't do that kind of trivial stuff any more."

"It's not trivial," he said, casting Anna Marie a wary look. "But no, I don't usually do it. This was a special case."

Anna Marie folded her arms and made her tone nonchalant. "Yes, I'm just a special case. There's nothing more to it than that." When Desmond narrowed his gaze, she took a hasty step back. "I'd better leave you two alone and, um…get back to my lunch." She turned and left.

Once she reached the dining room, Anna Marie fell into a chair and closed her eyes. For the first time in her life, she hated her sister. She hated her elegant manners, her height—five foot eleven compared to her five foot three—and her degrees. But she mostly hated the fact that her sister had had Desmond in the most intimate way—a way Anna Marie knew she never would.

She rubbed her temples, determined not to imagine what they were saying to each other. It had all been so perfect. Too perfect. Now it was over. Suddenly, she heard footsteps approaching. She picked up her fork, pretending to eat. "That was fast, Tracie," she said, staring at the food on her plate. "Is he gone?"

"No, he's not gone," Desmond said.

Anna Marie looked up at him, alarmed. "What are you doing here?" she said in a harsh voice. "Where's Tracie?"

"She's getting something from her car." He casually pulled out the chair beside her and sat.

Anna Marie jumped to her feet. "What are you doing? You can't stay here."

"Sure I can. Tracie invited me to lunch. Something you neglected to do." He reached for the chicken salad. "Could you get me a plate and a fork?"

"You should leave."

He slid her plate over to him. "Okay, we'll share."

Anna Marie turned. "I'll get you a plate." She went into the kitchen and seconds later returned with a plate, knife and fork and a glass. "I don't think this is a good idea."

"Why?"

"Because—" She stopped when Tracie appeared in the doorway.

"Desmond's staying for lunch," she said in a bright voice. "Isn't that wonderful?" She reached across the table, briefly covered his hand with hers and smiled at him.

Anna Marie turned away. "Yes, wonderful."

"Why are you sitting over there? Sit by me."

Desmond poured grape juice into his glass. "I'm comfortable where I am."

Anna Marie saw Tracie frown and said, "I'm sure he'd prefer to look at you instead of me."

Tracie's smile returned; Desmond stiffened and set the pitcher down with a bang.

Tracie smoothed her hair. "I remember when we were first dating you couldn't keep your eyes off me. I guess some things never change."

Desmond picked up his fork, then set it back down. "Look, Tracie, there's something I have to tell you. I'm more than Anna Marie's lawyer. Ow!" He glared at Anna Marie and rubbed his shin where she'd kicked him.

"Are you okay?" Tracie asked.

"Yes," he grumbled, sending Anna Marie a fierce look.

Anna Marie patted him on the shoulder. "It's probably a leg cramp." Anna Marie lifted her knife. "I know they can be very painful and unexpected."

Tracie cut a tomato slice. "What were you telling me about you and Anna Marie?"

Anna Marie made a dismissive gesture with her hand. "It's just business, nothing to concern you."

"That's where you're wrong," Desmond said. "Because Anna Marie and I are—" He suddenly swore and grabbed his arm. When he removed his hand, blood stained his palm.

Anna Marie glanced down at the knife which she'd used to jab him. She swallowed, then said in a small voice, "I'm sorry."

"You're so clumsy," Tracie said, grabbing a bunch of napkins and handing them to Desmond.

Desmond pushed the chair back with such force it made a loud squeak as it scraped against the floor. He stood, keeping his voice low. "Excuse me."

Tracie jumped to her feet, ready to help him, but he shook his head. "No, you stay here. Anna Marie, show me where you keep your first-aid kit."

From the look in his eyes, she knew best not to argue.

Chapter 12

"I can't believe you stabbed me," Desmond said as he sat on the edge of the bathtub while Anna Marie cleaned his wound with hydrogen peroxide. She then dabbed on an antibiotic ointment and covered the wound with a small bandage.

"I'm really sorry. I didn't mean to jab that hard."

"Why did you lie?" he said in a hard tone.

Anna Marie returned the first-aid items to the kit. "I didn't lie. I am a client of yours."

"You're more than that and I was trying to tell Tracie before you became violent."

"You can't tell her."

"Why not?"

"Because she's my sister."

"So what?"

"And she still loves you. She wants you back."

He started to laugh.

"You think that's funny?"

"Yes, I also know it's impossible. Especially since…never mind. The point is we need to tell her the truth."

"I don't—"

Desmond surged to his feet. "I'm not going to pretend there's nothing between us. And—" He stopped and frowned. "Why did you flinch like that?"

"Like what?"

"Like I was going to hit you."

"No." She waved her hands. "I wasn't flinching, I was just reacting."

"Yes, you did," he said in a grim tone. "As though I was about to slap you across the face or something." He seized her arms and looked into her eyes with such tenderness that she had to look away. "I have a temper, but I've never hit a woman in my life. And I swear to you that I'd never hurt you." He then cupped her face, his hands warm against her skin, and for a moment Anna Marie brushed her cheek against them, feeling his strength and knowing he'd never use it against her. He sighed. "It's at times like this that I wish I knew more about you." He let his hands fall. "Why won't you tell me about your past?"

"Because it's not that interesting. I know you'd never hurt me, it was just reflex. No big deal."

Desmond shut his eyes and rested his head against the door. "Anna Marie, don't do this to me." He opened his eyes and held out his hand. "Every time I think I have a hold of you—" he closed his hand "—you somehow slip free." He opened his hand.

"I don't know what you mean."

He leaned against the sink. "Do we have something special here or don't we? I think we do, but that doesn't matter because I'm not the one trying to lie."

"I don't want to lie, but—"

He wrapped an arm around her waist. "So you agree we have something special?"

"Yes."

He wrapped his other arm around her waist and lowered his head. "And you don't want to lose it?" He placed a kiss behind her ear.

Her body responded to the gentle pressure of his mouth as though he'd switched on a button. "No." She took a deep breath, but it didn't stop her pulse from pounding. "I don't want to lose it."

He nuzzled her neck. "So we have to tell Tracie the truth."

"But—"

Desmond straightened and looked at her. "I know she's your sister and my ex-wife. That makes the situation awkward, weird and, er...strange, but we're not doing anything illegal. We're adults. She'll understand."

Anna Marie dropped her gaze, unconvinced.

He turned to the door. "I'll tell her."

"No. Not now." She pulled on his arm, realizing too late that it was the wounded one when Desmond winced. She immediately let go. "I'm sorry."

"You're going to pay for this," he softened his words with a teasing grin.

"Is everything okay?" Tracie said on the other side of the door. She tried the knob. "Did you know the door is locked? Is that safe?"

"We're fine," Anna Marie said.

"Oh. I didn't think bandaging a wound would take that long."

"We're almost done," Desmond said, then lowered his voice. "When do you want me to tell her?"

Anna Marie rubbed her hands together, unsure. "I'll tell her later."

"When?"

"Soon, but not today. Enough has happened. I haven't seen her in years. I didn't even know she'd been married, much less divorced, and then you show up. I just need time to recover."

"Okay. You promise me you'll tell her?"

"Yes," Anna Marie said, then opened the bathroom door and left before he could probe further. Tracie stood in the hallway with her hands on her hips looking annoyed.

"What happened?" she demanded. "You were in there forever."

"The bandage kept unraveling," Anna Marie said.

Desmond nodded. "Sort of like a lie. They tend to do that."

"Only when they're not done right," she shot back.

"Then maybe you shouldn't try." He walked past her and returned to the dining room.

They all settled down to lunch again when Tracie brought up the subject Anna Marie had hoped to avoid.

"Desmond, what were you telling me about you and Anna Marie earlier?"

"That he's also my financial adviser," Anna Marie said before he could speak. "We've been discussing the cost of repairs to this place."

Tracie turned to him. "Is that why you stopped by?"

Desmond's jaw twitched. "One of the reasons, but let's eat. I'm tired of talking."

"It's fate," Tracie said as she and Anna Marie walked in the back garden after Desmond had gone. "I was meant to see him again. You like him, don't you?"

Anna Marie shoved her hands in her pockets. "Yes, he's very nice."

"And smart and handsome and—"

"Yes, he's all those things."

"Will you help me get him back?"

Anna Marie kicked a pebble out of her path. "I don't think I can."

"Why not? Just tell him how much you care about me and tell him all my good qualities."

"He married you. Wouldn't he already know that?"

"Sometimes a man needs reminding."

Anna Marie stopped and looked at her. "The thing is I—"

Tracie looped her arm through her sister's, forcing her to walk again. "I know it's unfair of me to drag you into my private affairs. I'm just glad to be here with you again. Forget I said anything."

Anna Marie glanced up at the trees. *I wish I could.*

At dinner Anna Marie pushed food around her plate, unable to eat as the afternoon's events continued to replay in her mind.

"Are you coming down with something?" Jane asked anxiously.

She scooped up some peas. "No, I'm fine."

"Your sister's visit bothered you, didn't it?" Leona said.

"And that man," Gerald added.

Anna Marie set her fork down, ready to lie, but one look at their earnest, caring expressions forced her to change her mind. She was used to telling lies or hiding the truth, but tonight she didn't want to. She clasped her hands together and told them all that had happened. When she was done, Leona stared at her, openmouthed, Jane wiped her forehead with a napkin and Gerald gave a low whistle.

Jane nodded. "That's quite a mess."

"So when will you tell her?" Leona asked.

Anna Marie shrugged. "Soon. I have to choose the right moment."

Gerald lifted his glass and jerked it toward her to emphasize his point, spilling some of his juice. "Make it quick, that way it won't hurt too much. It's like removing a Band-Aid."

Jane took her napkin and cleaned up the minor spill. "Yes, that sounds like a good idea. Do it as soon as you can."

Anna Marie nodded. "I know, but I feel guilty."

"Why?"

"Because she still loves him."

"Don't you?"

"I don't know—"

"Yes, you do," Leona said with a smug grin. "It's written all over your face. You love him so don't let him go. She had him once, but he wants you now."

Gerald shook his head in amazement. "He's certainly a lucky man to have two women who want him."

Anna Marie laughed. "That's nothing new for Desmond. You should have seen him in high school."

Jane leaned forward, her eyes bright with curiosity. "You've known him since high school?"

Anna Marie squirmed in her seat. "Sort of. I mean, I knew him in high school, then lost touch until a few months ago."

"How did your sister meet him?"

"I don't know. I didn't ask."

"I'm sure it doesn't matter," Leona said.

"I was just curious," Jane said. "It seems strange to me."

"Me, too," Anna Marie admitted.

Jane looked pensive. "Almost too much of a coincidence."

"What do you mean by that?"

She shook her head. "I don't know. I was just thinking that it's odd. Of all the men in the world, your sister married your high-school crush?"

"Stranger things have happened," Leona said.

"Yes," Anna Marie said. "Tracie never knew how I felt about him. She didn't even know who he was. She didn't go to the same school I did and she's five years younger than I am. We only reconnected after I'd left school. It's just one of those things."

"A real mess," Gerald said.

The phone rang and Jane left to answer it, then came back and whispered, "It's him." She handed Anna Marie the phone.

Anna Marie looked at the group, crossed her fingers, then left the dining room. "Hi," she said.

"I was wondering how you were doing."

"I should be asking you that question."

"The doctor said I get to keep my arm," he teased.

Anna Marie walked into the living room and laid on the couch. "I truly am sorry about that."

"Don't worry. You'll make it up to me on our date."

She sat up. "What?"

"I'm coming by this Saturday for breakfast, remember? Then I'm taking you out."

"Yes, I remember." Anna Marie rested her head against the back of the couch and stared up at the ceiling, trying to keep the note of panic from her voice. A daytime date with Desmond. She was a creature of the night who never felt safe in the day. What would they do? Where would they go? What would they talk about? Would he still find her appealing? "I'm looking forward to it," she said, trying to sound enthusiastic. "Where are you taking me?"

"It's a surprise."

Chapter Thirteen

"So what exactly do you do?" Anna Marie overheard Gerald ask Desmond while they sat in the living room as Leona finished cooking breakfast.

"I'm a lawyer."

"And what are your intentions?"

Anna Marie groaned and hurried to the kitchen, not wanting to hear the answer. "I hope breakfast is almost ready," she told Leona. "If I leave Desmond alone with Gerald any longer, he might run away."

"He looks like a man who can handle himself and Gerald is only asking because he cares about you."

"About me?"

"Yes, we all do." Leona straightened Anna Marie's necklace. "You look really nice."

Anna Marie smiled. She'd chosen her outfit carefully and wore a tailored white lace blouse, a pair of jean shorts, a pair of striped stockings and leather boots. Leona had loaned her the necklace. She was still amazed by how much had changed in her relationship with Leona, Gerald and Jane in only a few weeks. Although they all told her how nice she looked, she'd worried about Desmond's reaction. Would he think it appropriate for a daytime date? When she opened the door, Desmond's look erased that fear. He undressed her with one look that made her blush from head to toe. She was used to such a blatant assessment in the evening, but in the day his gaze was even more potent. At that moment she realized that even without the night magic of Malika, Anna Marie could fill a man with desire.

"No, don't go," he said when she turned to go inside. "I like looking at you."

"The others are waiting."

He rested his hand on the doorframe and let his gaze dip to her legs. "Let them wait. I'm enjoying this."

She shook her head in disbelief. "Come on."

She turned to leave and he whistled with appreciation.

"That angle is even better."

Before she could reply, he followed her inside and she introduced him to Leona and Jane. Although they were polite, she still wondered how things would turn out.

"I hope this breakfast won't be a disaster," she said.

"Relax," Leona said in a reassuring tone. "I'm sure it will be fine."

The breakfast was better than fine. A feast of dishes fought for space on the table—seasoned vegetarian omelets, mini-meat tarts, whole-wheat bagels, beef sausages and hash browns smothered in gravy. And as for the company, Desmond dazzled them all. He charmed Jane and Leona and by the time they had finished eating, he had Gerald patting him on the back as though he were a long-lost son. Anna Marie watched, amazed by the ease of the conversation and laughter.

No one would suspect Desmond had a tattoo under his fine blue shirt, that he liked to drink beer from the bottle and that in high school he spent more time in detention than regular classes. He'd become a new man and had freed himself from his past. Something Anna Marie wanted. She kept her envy at bay, knowing that in a few months she'd leave Virginia and her past—erasing memories of foster homes and ten years as an exotic dancer. She would open a dance studio and teach the art of dance to build self-esteem to young girls and boys. And she'd leave this....

Anna Marie looked around the table and felt an

odd pain at the thought of leaving her new friends behind. *Friends.* She'd never used that word before, but that's who they were to her and she would miss them. Gerald's gruff responses, Jane's sweet replies, Leona's cooking and Desmond's everything: his looks, his smile, his touch, his laugh, his body.

Anna Marie brushed that thought aside. She didn't think about the future; she never had and she wouldn't start. Now was all that mattered.

"You were quiet at breakfast," Desmond said as he and Anna Marie left the house.

"I was just thinking."

"About what?"

"How happy everyone looked."

He rested an arm on her shoulders. "I'm glad you're not lonely anymore. I like them."

"And they like you."

"Have you told Tracie?"

"I left her a message to call me. I'll tell her then."

He nodded. "Good."

Anna Marie started to speak when she saw it— a beautiful chrome and leather machine with sleek lines. Desmond noticed her gaze and smiled, patting his motorcycle. "I thought you'd like a ride."

"You know me too well."

"I intend to know you better."

She took the helmet he handed her. "Where are we going?"

"That's a surprise, too." He straddled the bike.

She did the same. "You can't give me a hint?"

"I can, but I'm not going to. Hold on tight."

She wrapped her arms around his waist. "With pleasure."

Seconds later, Anna Marie discovered the reckless joy that could be found on the back of motorcycle. The rush of the wind, the feel of the road. She was almost disappointed when they reached their destination. She got off, then looked around and noticed they were in a church parking lot and saw a sign that read Church Bazaar. She saw a moonbounce, clowns and vendors. The scent of hamburgers and hot dogs drifted toward them amid the sound of laughter and conversations. "What are we doing here? Even if it is a bazaar, you don't strike me as the church-going type."

Desmond took her hand and walked toward the bustling crowd, admiring the colorful stalls, families and children running about. "I'm not, but my parents are here."

Anna Marie halted. "Your parents? You want me to meet your parents? That's the surprise?"

He turned to her. "I knew that if I asked you to meet them, you would say no."

"So you tricked me."

"You're surprised, aren't you? See? I kept my promise."

Anna Marie looked down at her shorts and fishnets with dismay. "But I'm not dressed to meet them."

He took her hand and started to walk. "You look great."

She held back. "Please, let me meet them another time."

"I've been seeing you about three months. It's time."

She tried to pull her hand free. "Maybe—"

"You seem to have a problem walking. Do you want me to pick you up and carry you?"

"No," she said with outrage. "Stay away from me."

"Then come on."

Anna Marie sighed in defeat. "I'm not really good at family events."

"Relax. This is a casual atmosphere so you won't feel pressured."

"Wow, the bazaar is pretty big," Anna Marie said, surprised by the many vendors she saw lining the lawn once inside the bazaar.

"Yes. The church holds it annually for the community and the food's great so don't be shy." He glanced around. "I don't see them."

"Are they expecting me?"

"No, I'm going to surprise them, too." He handed her two twenty-dollar bills. "Get some food and I'll find you," he said, then left before she could protest.

Anna Marie stood there for a moment wondering what she should do with herself, then she noticed a vendor selling bamboo place mats and thought of Jane.

"They're handmade," the vendor said.

"They're lovely." She bought a set of four, then noticed someone selling clear acrylic paperweights with exquisite carvings inside and bought one for Gerald. She then bought a crocheted earring and necklace set for Leona and a Swiss Army knife for Desmond.

She was busy looking at a hand-painted silk scarf, with an image of a white orchid, when someone behind her said, "It looks too old for you."

Anna Marie turned and saw a stern older man with white hair, mocha skin and piercing dark eyes. She placed the scarf down and picked up another one, hoping he would go away. "It's not for me, it's for a friend."

"I see." He cast a cursory glance at her outfit. "I didn't think it would be your style."

"You'd be surprised. My style is eclectic."

He lifted an eyebrow but didn't comment, then he glanced at her bags. "I see you've been busy."

"Yes."

The vendor smiled. "She bought two of my scarves, Pastor."

Pastor? This cold-looking man with the intimidating gaze was a pastor? He'd be better suited as a prison warden. She could imagine him terrorizing his congregation with some damning message.

He touched one of the scarves with his long, elegant fingers. "I've never seen you before. Usually this event brings the familiar group. However, it's always nice to see a new face."

Anna Marie made a noncommittal sound, not sure she believed him. Although his words were kind, his tone was cool. "Thank you." She turned and saw Desmond coming toward her with a handsome older man at his side. It was evident the other man had given Desmond his build and walk. She also noticed a third individual who looked familiar.

It took Anna Marie a moment to place her, then she remembered. Dana, Desmond's cousin—the one who had driven them back from HH. She looked the same; her youthful glow had matured into a beautiful presence. Although Anna Marie was terrified of meeting Desmond's father, she was glad to have an excuse to leave the pastor. She picked up her bags. "I'd better go."

Dana reached her before she could. "Anna Marie Williams! When Desmond told me you were here, I had to see for myself. I can't believe it's you." She hugged her.

Anna Marie hugged her back, pleased to see her again. "Yes, it's me. You look great."

"Thanks."

Desmond grinned. "And I see you've already met my father."

Anna Marie began to hold her hand out to the

man standing next to him, then realized Desmond was staring at the man next to *her.*

"No, we haven't been formally introduced," the man said. "I'm Pastor Rockwell. Who are you?"

His father was a pastor? Anna Marie found it difficult to recover as she sat with Desmond's family at a covered picnic table. She'd discovered the other man was his uncle and his mother joined them shortly afterward. Mrs. Rockwell was a thin woman with a face as charming as her husband's was stern. Anna Marie wondered how they'd managed to stay married so long.

"It's a pleasure to meet you, Anna Marie," Mrs. Rockwell said. "You're a nice change from some of the women Desmond has introduced to us before."

"There haven't been that many," Desmond said, handing Anna Marie a slice of his apple.

"There have been plenty," his mother said with a knowing grin. "But at least now you have a nice good girl."

Desmond winked at Anna Marie. "Yes, she's very good."

Mrs. Rockwell shook her head. "Oh, the trouble he used to get into." She lifted her gaze to the sky. "Good Lord."

"That's because of the crowd he was running with," Pastor Rockwell said. "A bad crowd. But he's done well and made us proud." He sent his son a look that softened his face, cracking the austere veneer, and made Desmond smile.

Anna Marie noticed the exchange and sensed that their relationship was close. She could see that Desmond loved his father and his father's words and respect meant a lot to him. There was a strong bond. She didn't know anything about bonds like that but could always spot them with envy.

Dana stood up from her seat at the other end of the table and came up to her. She nudged her shoulder. "Let's go for a walk."

Anna Marie looked at Desmond, unsure. He grinned and she gathered her courage and left.

The two women walked in silence at first, then Dana said, "I'm glad you're back in his life."

"Back? I was never really in it. At least not for long."

"I know, but there's something about him that's different when you're around. You're certainly an improvement to the others."

"Have there been many?" Anna Marie couldn't help asking, although she already knew the answer.

"Enough, but I don't have to tell you. You know."

She rubbed her arm. "So I guess he hasn't changed."

"He's changed in all the right ways. He and his father used to fight all the time. Now that Desmond's mellowed, they're a lot happier. I was worried at one time that it would end."

"Why?"

"When he divorced, Uncle didn't believe in it. They really liked his ex."

"Oh."

"I'm only telling you this in case you find my uncle a little cold. He can be. Especially when he thinks Desmond is 'going astray,' as he likes to call it. He thought Tracie was the perfect woman for his son and hasn't quite reconciled himself to the fact that it's over."

"Why did it end?"

"He hasn't told you?" Dana said, surprised.

She shook her head.

"Then I certainly won't."

"Do you think he still loves his ex?"

"No, but he's always felt guilty that his divorce hurt his father and he wouldn't want to do anything to hurt him again. I'm glad you're with him and in time they'll see it, too."

Anna Marie wasn't sure she wanted them to. She knew she wasn't the type of woman they'd approve of. Desmond's father didn't look like a man easy to please. She'd had a foster father like him once and she hadn't been able to please him, either. But she knew it didn't matter because her relationship with Desmond was just for a time and it would end. Throughout her life, relationships always ended and she didn't expect anything different.

"We'll see."

* * *

"Well?" Desmond asked his father as they sat alone at the table. His mother and uncle had gone back to the bazaar and he looked at Anna Marie and Dana walking in the distance.

"Well what?"

"What did you think?"

Pastor Rockwell rested his arms on the table, his voice low. "Do you really want to know?"

"Yes."

"I think you should patch things up with Tracie."

Desmond rubbed the back of his neck and groaned. "Dad, we've had this discussion."

"Then we should have it again."

"It's not going to happen."

"I know things went bad, but it is a man's duty to forgive. She is a good woman. She is right for you. She came from a good home and had a good education."

"You sound like a snob. I bet you think heaven has a hierarchy."

"I know what makes a good wife. I have nothing against your current young woman."

"Don't talk about her like that," Desmond said in a sharp voice.

His father raised his brows innocently. "Like what?"

"As though she were some chick I picked up off the street."

"You've come close before."

Desmond tapped the side of his glass, his gaze turning dark. "That was before."

"Yes, and I want you to remember that. Look at what she's wearing."

"I like what she's wearing. There's nothing wrong with it."

"No, you wouldn't think so," his father said in disgust. "But you have to remember that you're not the man you once were. I don't dislike Anne Mary—"

"Anna Marie."

"Right. I don't dislike her personally, but she's a reminder of your past. A past that you've left behind."

"Yes, I've left it behind."

"But has she?"

Desmond paused. "What?"

"What has she been doing these past few years? She was once a thief, spent time in that halfway house. You told me she ran away from her last foster home. Who is she?"

"You just met her."

"That's not enough. You know what I mean."

"Dad, she is a good woman. Don't judge her so harshly. She's got a lot of heart. Before she found out about her inheritance, she had a great government job with the Virginia Department of Health and Human Services. And you should see how she interacts with the residents who live in her boarding house."

"She lives in a boarding house? The only boarding houses I know about are not in the best part of town. Actually, I didn't know any existed. Besides, the kind of people who need to pay for a room in such establishments are usually not from the higher sector of town."

"It's a nice area," Desmond said with a tired sigh. "We've both become different people and that's who you need to see."

"What did she do after she ran away?"

Desmond let his gaze fall. "I don't know."

"How many foster homes has she lived in?"

"I don't know."

"Has she ever been caught shoplifting again?"

"I don't know."

"And yet you *know* she's changed? You trust her?"

Desmond maintained his father's gaze. "Yes."

"Come on, Desmond. You're not a stupid man. You're a rich man. You're a prize to someone like her. You have to be careful. I would start to wonder why she hasn't told you everything about herself. What is she hiding?"

"She's not hiding anything."

"And yet you know so much about her," he scoffed.

"She's been hurt and it takes time for her to trust people."

"I've seen you make mistakes before, Desmond—"

"I know," he said in a bitter voice. "And you judged me for every one."

"And forgave you."

Desmond pounded the table. "They're the same. All my life you've been my judge *and* my jury."

"Only because I knew the man you could be. The man you are now, and I don't want that to change." His father glanced at Anna Marie in the distance. "I don't want anyone to change it. Be careful. Secrets are dangerous things."

Chapter 14

"Your father didn't like me," Anna Marie said as they sat on her front porch watching the sunset. Dana had offered to drop off Anna Marie's purchases tomorrow since they wouldn't fit on the motorcycle. Anna Marie thanked her, then said goodbye to Desmond's uncle and parents before leaving.

Desmond was quiet a moment, leaning back on his elbows as he stared at the passing traffic, then said, "Sometimes it takes a while for my father to warm up to people."

"Seems like an odd trait for a pastor."

"It is," he admitted with a grin. "But he has a firm belief of what he thinks is right and wrong."

"You must have driven him crazy."

His grin widened. "I had my moments."

"Maybe if you'd told me about him, I could have—"

He turned to her. "Could have what? Dressed differently, acted differently?" He shook his head, determined. "No, I wanted you to be exactly as you are. And he's going to get to know you and love you as much as I—" He stopped and leaned forward, resting his elbows on his knees. "As much as he needs to."

"Dana told me that your parents loved Tracie."

"They did."

"And they want the two of you to get back together."

"They do, but that's never going to happen."

"Why did you divorce?"

He sent her a sly glance. "When you tell Tracie about us, I'll tell you."

"Hmm."

"When are you going to tell her?"

"I told you I left a message. I'll tell her soon."

"I want to believe you."

"But you don't?"

"Only because I still know so little about you."

Anna Marie scratched the back of her hand, annoyed. "What do you need to know?"

"What song did you like as a child? What was your mother like? Where was your first foster home? Do you have a hobby?"

"Oh, I get it. Your father has cast some doubts about me. No wonder he liked Tracie. Her life was an open book and pleasant to listen to. Something so happy and great. No wonder she likes talking about it all the time. Unfortunately, I don't. I want to forget mine."

"Why? Your experiences, whether good or bad, make you who you are. I want to know what you like, what you dislike. If you ever have nightmares. What you're afraid of. I want to know everything I can about you."

Anna Marie stood, eager to end the conversation. "I'm thirsty. Are you? I can go get us something."

Desmond stared up at her, his expression grim. "If this is just a game to you, then let's stop it now."

"Break up?" her voice cracked.

"Yes. I'm too old for flashy relationships that don't mean anything. I've had them and I'm over them. I want a real woman and I want a real relationship. And that means honesty. That means telling Tracie the truth. That means letting me know more about you. But if that's not what you want, tell me now."

Anna Marie folded her arms, wishing she could, but knowing it was too dangerous. She never revealed specifics of her past. Why did he need to know all that stuff? It was something she couldn't give him. Anna Marie hung her head in defeat.

He stood: "Fine."

She heard the finality of his words and then his

footsteps against the gravel drive. Within minutes he would be gone and she'd never see him again. And for the first time in her life, she fought her fear of judgment and called out to him. "'One Thousand and One Nights.'"

He turned around. "What?"

"'One Thousand and One Nights.' That was one of my favorite stories growing up."

He walked toward her and Anna Marie gripped the railing to maintain her strength. "I once had this illustrated edition I got from a used bookstore and I would imagine myself as one of the characters in the many tales of fantasy. I would close my eyes and ride the magic carpet and dream of the wishes I would tell a genie if I had one. It was my favorite book."

Desmond stopped in front of her. "What happened to it?"

"My book?"

He nodded.

Anna Marie swallowed. "I don't remember."

He covered her hand with his and said in a soft voice, "Yes, you do."

She stared down at their hands, feeling his warmth and caring. "It got burned," she said in a flat voice.

"How?"

Anna Marie looked at him. "My foster father threw it in the fireplace. He wasn't an awful man and I'm sure he didn't mean to. He didn't know how much it meant to me. He just saw me reading instead of doing my chores, so he took the book and burned it. I watched as each beautiful page curled and turn black."

"What did you do after that?"

"I did my chores." She lightened her voice. "But I survived. Always have." She shrugged. "So now you know something more about me."

"Thank you." He lifted her hand and held it to his chest. "And I'll make sure you never regret trusting me."

His fervent words and piercing gaze were too much for her. Too intimate. Too much of a bond that she'd never had with anyone. "Now it's your turn. There's something more I want to learn about you."

"What?"

She lifted his sleeve. "I know you have this tattoo. But I've never taken the time to find the other one."

"Do you want me to tell you?"

She took his hand and walked to the front door. "No, I'd prefer to look for it."

"It might be hard to find," he teased.

She opened the door then sent him a seductive glance. "I'm very patient."

Anna Marie already knew where it was, but enjoyed pretending to find it. Desmond enjoyed it, too, and made an expedition of finding hidden places on her body, also. His tongue caressed her nipples, his hands lightly traced a path over her skin, seeking and finding her pleasure points. His mouth covered hers, slow and hot. He drew away and stared at her in wonder.

"Why?" he asked in a hoarse whisper.

"Why what?"

"Why do you make me feel this way?"

The corner of her mouth kicked up in a coy smile. "Because I'm good?"

Anna Marie expected him to smile at her teasing tone, but he didn't. Instead his eyes blazed down into hers. "No, there's something else. With you I feel..." He shook his head, frustrated that he couldn't find the words. "As though I'm a good person. You never judge me. That's what I remember most about you. When they handcuffed me, you didn't look at me with surprise or disappointment or disgust or anything, unlike—"

"Unlike your father?"

"You'd think he'd be happy that my brother and sister are perfect. They're both married with kids and have good jobs."

"Are you still practicing because of your father?"

Desmond was silent a moment, then said, "He doesn't want me to be idle. He thinks having a lawyer in the family is a good thing. That it will keep me responsible."

"But do you like it?"

"I'd quit it in a minute, but I'll stay for now."

"What do you want?"

He grinned and cupped her bottom. "Right now, I have what I want."

"Be serious."

He placed a kiss on her shoulder. "I am."

She teased the nipple on his chest. "What do you want, besides me?"

He covered her hand. "I haven't thought about it."

"You should."

His mouth twitched in amusement. "Dad's right about you. You're dangerous. That's what I like most."

"And that's what he worries about most."

His amusement died. "I didn't try to get into trouble, but there's just something in me that rebels."

"Fortunately, now you're close with your dad. You have a good relationship."

"I walk a tightrope and he's just waiting for me to fall off so he can judge me again." He rubbed his eyes. "Once he didn't talk to me for a year."

Anna Marie heard the pain in Desmond's voice and sought to offer him comfort. She caressed the side of his face. "He loves you, though."

"Only because he has to."

"I don't."

"You don't what?"

"I don't have to love you, but I do." She hadn't meant to tell him, but the remote tone in his voice tore at her. He didn't speak, and fear swept through her as she remembered the many times she'd gotten too close to someone only to have them reject her. She let her gaze fall, no longer able to look at him, then he touched her side, making her skin tingle. He'd touched her many times before but somehow this was different and he whispered her name in a way she'd never heard before—more intimate—and when he kissed her, she felt as though they were one; that their relationship had changed and deepened.

For the first time, they didn't have sex, they made love—they went beyond the physical pursuit of pleasure and let their hearts become involved. It made every touch, every look and every kiss more tender. When they were through they lay in bed, surprised by the magnitude of their feelings.

Desmond reached for the phone. "I want you to call Tracie."

"Now?"

"Yes."

"I told you I left a message."

"Leave another one."

Anna Marie took the phone from him and dialed. When the voice mail came on, she said, "Tracie, it's Anna Marie again. Please call me. It's important." She handed the phone back to Desmond. "Does that please you?"

"Now call her cell phone."

"What if she answers?"

"That's the point, isn't it? Unless you've been calling her house knowing that she usually lets it go to voice mail."

"That's not why. Okay?"

He nodded to the phone. "I'm waiting."

She dialed, then waited, silently praying that the voice mail would kick in. It didn't.

"Hello?" Tracie said.

"Tracie? It's Anna Marie. I've been trying to reach you."

"I know. Sorry, I've been traveling. Right now I'm in New York."

"Oh, well, there's something I need to tell you."

"Okay, but make it quick. We might lose the connection."

"I'm seeing Desmond. He's here with me right now."

"That's great. It's like you've read my mind. I've been trying to reach him, but he won't return any of my calls, but he can't ignore me now. Give him the phone."

"No, wait. That's not what I meant."

"You can explain later. Please let me talk to him before I lose this connection."

"He's in my bedroom."

"I don't care where he is. Go and get him."

Anna Marie covered the mouthpiece. "She wants to talk to you."

"Why?"

"Because she's been trying to reach you."

"I know."

"Please."

He reluctantly took the receiver. "Did you hear what Anna Marie just told you? We're see-ing…What? Tracie, don't start that with me." He briefly closed his eyes and softly swore. "Tracie? Tracie, will you list—I'm trying to—" He turned off the phone and threw it across the room. It hit the far wall and shattered into pieces. Desmond covered his eyes. "I'll buy you another one."

Anna Marie kissed his shoulder. "*Now* you know why I leave messages. It's almost impossible to get Tracie to listen over the phone."

He let his hand fall. "I'd forgotten about that."

"I told you I'd tell her and I will. She's away right now anyway. I'll talk to her when she comes back."

Desmond lay back for a moment, then sniffed the air. "Hmm, something smells good."

"Probably dinner," Anna Marie said, recogniz-ing the aromatic result of Leona's cooking.

"I'll stay."

"You haven't been invited."

He stood and began to dress. "So invite me." He pulled on his shirt. "Or I'll invite myself."

Anna Marie knew she couldn't win so she also dressed without saying anything. Gerald, Jane and Leona enjoyed Desmond at dinner as much as they had at breakfast, if not more. Afterward they all went into the family room and played a board game, then watched a movie on cable. By eleven o'clock, the residents said good-night then headed for bed. Anna Marie stood, ready to walk Desmond to the door, but he took her hand in a warm clasp and stopped her. "Do you think you'll be lonely tonight?" he asked in a deep tone.

"No," she said with an edge of regret. "I'm really tired."

"Me, too." He held up his free hand when she began to speak. "I don't want anything," he said his dark eyes searching her face. "I just want to be with you."

Anna Marie froze in confusion. "You just want to be with me?"

Desmond ran a tired hand down his face, still holding hers with his other one. "Look, what I just said is soppy enough. Please don't make me repeat it. Can I stay or not?"

She drew her hand away from his hold and a coy smile touched her lips. "I'll bolt the front door and meet you upstairs."

Anna Marie woke up alone, filled with an unquenchable joy. Last night had been all she could have hoped for. She still felt Desmond's arms around her as he held her close before he fell asleep. There was no pretense, no demands, just the pleasure of being together. She didn't care that he'd be gone in the morning; the night was all she needed.

When she woke she reached over as she always did to touch the space beside her. His side of the bed was empty, but still warm. Anna Marie swept her hand over the empty space, surprised. Usually it was cold by now. She paused when she heard a deep rumbling voice. She sat up and saw Desmond sitting on the end of the bed feeding a piece of lettuce to Nika. He'd put on a pair of jeans, but his back was bare.

Anna Marie blinked, then reached out to touch him to make sure he was real. She snatched back her hand before she did. He continued to talk to Nika in a low tone but she couldn't make out the words. Not that her addled brain could process anything. He was still here. He hadn't gone. He'd been with her all day and all night. She hadn't had to pretend or be someone else. The sight of him made her giddy with joy. She pushed the sheets aside and wrapped her arms around his neck, inhaling his scent. He smelled clean, like freshly laundered sheets.

"You smell good," she said.

"I used your shower."

She kissed his shoulder, then behind his ear. "I'm so happy you're here."

"Same." He chuckled, amused by her exuberance. "Good morning."

Anna Marie jumped out of bed and grabbed her robe before heading to the bathroom with a spring in her step. "Yes, it is."

Her good mood continued throughout breakfast and improved when Dana arrived that afternoon to drop off the gifts Anna Marie had purchased at the bazaar. Anna Marie introduced her to everyone, then handed out her purchases. The residents received them as though it were an unexpected holiday. They oohed and aahed like children, except for Desmond, who was oddly quiet as he stared at his Swiss Army knife.

"He likes it," Dana assured Anna Marie when she caught her worried expression. "You have a lovely house. Care to give me a tour?"

"Of course."

Anna Marie proudly showed Dana around the house, making sure to skip the basement, then invited her to stay for lunch. She did and they all enjoyed the food and friendship. Eventually, Dana said she had to go and Desmond said the same. Anna Marie reluctantly followed him to the door, wishing he would stay another night. "It's been fun."

"Yes." He held up his gift. "Thanks for this," he said in a neutral tone.

"You're welcome," she said, trying to read his eyes, but unable to. She folded her arms. "Is something wrong?"

"No. I'll call you." He bent and kissed her lightly on the mouth, then turned.

Anna Marie began to reply, but Jane called her seeking advice on how to wear her scarf, so Anna Marie went back inside.

Desmond headed for his motorcycle, but Dana stopped him. "You're really serious about her."

"I don't want to talk about it," he said in a tight voice. He walked around her.

"That's understandable. You were serious about Tracie, too."

"That was a mistake."

"My dad and your dad have been on the phone for hours talking about you."

He held up the knife. "Do you know how much this means to me? Years ago I told her I wanted one and I'd let myself forget about it, but she remembered." He cradled the knife in his hand and lowered his voice. "She remembered."

"I know she's important to you. And I like Anna Marie, but she's already causing you trouble."

Desmond stopped and rested his hands on his hips. "She hasn't done anything."

Dana tilted her head to the side. "If she'd only come dressed a little more conservative—"

He tapped his chest. "I like the way she dresses, how she looks and talks. I like everything about her and I don't care what anyone else thinks."

"If this is some sort of rebellion, you're winning."

"I'm not with Anna Marie to provoke my father. I'm too old for that."

"You hate your job, your ex and your apartment is all show. You pretend to love it, but the moment I saw you here—" she turned to the house "—you looked at home." She sighed and met his gaze. "I want you to be happy, just be careful because it's not only about you. Anna Marie hasn't had an easy life and exposing her to our family's rejection isn't fair to her."

"I'll protect her," he said as if he were willing to fight the world. "She'll be safe with me." He headed for his motorcycle then stopped and swore. He slowly spun around. "There's something else you should know."

"What?"

"Tracie's her sister."

"Your ex?"

He nodded grimly.

Dana burst into laughter, then sobered when she saw Desmond's face. "You're serious?"

He nodded again. She laughed harder.

"This isn't funny," he growled.

She wiped away tears. "I know and I'm sorry." She covered her mouth, trying to suppress her amusement.

"We haven't told her yet," Desmond said when Dana finally calmed down. "She's out of town right now, but Anna Marie will tell her when Tracie gets back."

Dana patted his shoulder with pity. "Desmond, Trouble definitely likes to follow you. And this time Trouble has a name."

Trouble returned six weeks later bearing gifts for Anna Marie.

"You have to change the decor in this room," Tracie said as she walked around Anna Marie's bedroom, her gaze falling on the ornate bed draped in red silk. "Why did you bring me up here anyway?"

"Because I want to talk to you."

"About what?"

Anna Marie began to reply when Tracie suddenly squealed and jumped on the bed. "What is it?"

Anna Marie looked around astonished. "What is what?"

Tracie waved her finger at the dresser. "That!"

Anna Marie turned and saw Nika peeking his head out. "Oh, that's just my turtle. He's harmless."

Tracie slowly crawled off the bed. "You have a turtle?"

"Yes. I'll explain more, later. Right now we have to talk."

"First, do you like what I got you?"

Anna Marie looked at the simple pants set her sister had purchased. She already knew it wouldn't fit and would spend the rest of its days in the back of her closet. "It's very thoughtful."

"I had to keep myself busy while I was away. It's all part of my strategy. They say absence makes the heart grow fonder, you know. I thought if I gave Desmond some distance after he saw me, he would miss me a bit. Now I'm going to put my strategy into action."

"Tracie, there's something I have to tell you."

Her sister's face fell. "You don't like the outfit I bought you. Don't worry, I can get you something else."

"No, it's not that."

"Good, because I think you have a scarf that will match it."

"It's about Desmond."

"Don't tell me, I know." She opened a drawer in search of the scarf. "He's seeing someone else, but that doesn't bother me. He might be seeing another woman, but he married me." She closed the drawer. "That's the difference."

"Yes, well the woman he's seeing is—"

Tracie opened another drawer, then stopped. "Oh, my goodness! Where did you get these?"

"They were gifts," Anna Marie said quickly, wishing she'd hidden them.

"Who sent them?"

"A friend," she said, uneasy.

Tracie pulled out Anna Marie's last pair of stockings. "Oh, it's a full-body one! This will look great on me. Can I borrow it?"

"No."

Tracie turned to her, surprised. Anna Marie had never denied her anything. "What?"

"No, you can't borrow them. Those are very special to me." She reached for them, but Tracie moved them out of her grasp.

She held them to her chest, affronted. "But we're sisters. You think I'll tear them or something?"

Anna Marie rubbed her hands, trying to find the right words to explain. But she couldn't tell her about the society. "No, it's just—"

"It's not like you to be selfish."

"I could help you find a similar pair."

Tracie thinned her lips. "I don't want a similar pair." She waved the stockings at her. "I want these."

"Well, I'm sorry, but you can't have them."

"Fine." She balled them up, shoved them back in the drawer then slammed the drawer shut.

"Let's get something to eat."

"I'm not hungry."

"Tracie, stop it. We're not going to fight over a simple pair of stockings. You know that I would let you have anything, but I want you to respect what I can't give you. There are so few things in my life that have been completely mine. Those stockings are one of those things." She took a deep breath. "And there's something else."

"Oh, no, bad news."

"In a sense. It's about Desmond—and me."

Tracie sniffed. "It's funny the way you say that, as though you were a couple or something." She giggled. "But that would never happen. You're not his type at all."

"You don't sound sure about that." Anna Marie folded her arms. "You're not as ditzy as you like to appear. You know what I've been trying to say."

"I've been trying to give you a chance to change your mind. I don't want you to make a fool of yourself."

"I've been able to handle myself without your help before."

"This isn't a pair of stockings, Anna Marie. Don't stand in my way."

"I don't plan to move."

"You don't have to because I know Desmond. He'll move on and leave you behind."

Anna Marie opened her mouth to respond, but someone knocked on the door and interrupted. She opened it and saw Leona.

"You'd better come. There's something wrong with Jane," she said.

Anna Marie ran downstairs and saw Jane lying on the couch. Gerald hovered over her.

"I'm fine," she said. "I had a fainting spell. That's all."

"Perhaps you should see a doctor," Anna Marie said.

"No, please. No doctors. I just felt light-headed.

You've been so good to us. I think there's something you should know. We—"

"Jane," Leona said. "You need to rest."

"But—"

"Just sleep, then you'll feel better." She sent Gerald a nervous look.

Anna Marie noticed the glance. Something more was going on, but she didn't want to pry.

"I'll take her to her room," Gerald said.

"It's okay if she stays here," Anna Marie said.

"Fine," Leona agreed. "I'll stay with her."

Anna Marie left the room. Secrets. They were all keeping secrets. She more than most. She was hiding so much—from the residents, from Desmond, from Tracie. No, that was wrong. Tracie knew about her and Desmond, but didn't care because she wanted Desmond and she always got what she wanted.

Anna Marie returned to her room, only to find that Tracie was gone. Minutes later she discovered the pair of stockings were gone, too.

Chapter 15

Her sister and the missing pair of stockings showed up three days later at an outdoor concert. Desmond and Anna Marie were enjoying a jazz band, food, wine and each other when Tracie showed up wearing full-body black silk stockings, which were clearly displayed through the cutouts in her dress.

"Isn't this a surprise?" Tracie said, coming over to them.

Desmond frowned. "What are you doing here? You hate these concerts."

"I didn't hate them. Is there any space on that blanket? I don't want to ruin my dress."

"No, there's no space."

Tracie looked at her sister. "You haven't said anything."

"I don't know what to say."

"You certainly don't have trouble with words at other times."

"Tracie," Anna Marie said in a tired voice. "Please don't do this."

"I'm not doing anything."

Desmond began to pack up their things. "Let's go."

"Oh, no. Don't do that. Anna Marie loves music. Especially music she can dance to."

Anna Marie seized her arm. "Don't—"

"Don't what?" Tracie asked in a cool voice. "Don't tell Desmond what you like to do?"

Desmond shook his head. "I don't know what you're trying to hint at, but I know a lot about Anna Marie. I know she loves music and dancing."

"And you know where she likes to do it?"

"Yes, we've gone to lots of clubs."

"So, I guess you know everything about her."

Anna Marie knew Tracie was getting ready to expose her. She stood and said, "Okay, let's talk." She grabbed her sister's arm and led her away.

"Where are you going?" Desmond asked as Anna Marie walked away.

"I'll be back. Tracie and I need to talk in private."

Tracie shrugged. "Okay."

Once they were a good distance away from Desmond, Anna Marie stopped and turned to her sister. "Why are you doing this?"

"You know why. I think it's very low of you to continue with this relationship when you *know* how I feel."

"Yes, I know how you feel, but I also know how he feels. If he gave me any indication that he wanted you back, I'd end the relationship."

"No, you wouldn't. You're only thinking about yourself."

"And that's why you stole my stockings? To punish me?"

"Hey, if you can take my husband, I can have your stupid stockings."

"He's not your husband anymore."

Tracie shook her head in pity. "Don't kid yourself, Anna Marie. How long have you had him? For a couple months? You've had your fun, but you can't keep him."

"I can try," Anna Marie said, although some doubt touched her heart.

Tracie scratched her side. "Have you met his father?"

"Yes."

Tracie paused, surprised, then recovered herself. "Then you know he's demanding."

"Yes, I know but—"

"Do you know that Desmond has always felt

guilty that he cost his father a prime position at another church? He had gotten in trouble with the law and the council passed over his father because of it. Desmond's been trying to make up for that ever since. And his father loves me. Despite everything."

"What happened?"

Tracie rolled her eyes and rubbed her arm. "It was a minor indiscretion. I was feeling lonely and it happened. Only once. I told Desmond, but he can be so stubborn. I mean, so I slept with a colleague. We all make mistakes."

"That's a big one."

Tracie's voice hardened. "Don't you dare judge me. You're far from perfect. I got Desmond's father to understand my failure and that I was very sorry. Just imagine if he ever found out about you."

"I told you what I did in confidence."

"Yes, but things can slip out. Yes, I wonder how Pastor Rockwell will feel knowing that you were an exotic dancer for ten years. That you'd once dated a guy who was arrested for burglary. What if I tell him about Mrs. Bell? Who she really was before she changed her identity. Better yet, what if he found out that she was the one who taught you how to dance?

"Oh, and then there are your residents. I did a little background check to find out more. Gerald spent eighteen years in prison for armed robbery.

Jane was a call girl and Leona dealt in the illegal prescription trade." She scratched the back of her neck. "What would he think then? He wants his son to interact with the right sort of people."

Tracie was right. Anna Marie knew she probably couldn't win this fight. Desmond loved his father and she wouldn't want to force him to choose. She knew the choice he would make. "Fine. It's over."

Tracie suddenly looked contrite. "I hope you understand why I had to do this. You only have a crush, which you'll get over. I love him."

Anna Marie paused. "What do you mean, I just have a crush?"

"You always have. You've had it for years and now you're living out a fantasy."

"Wait. I never told you about my crush on Desmond. How did you know?"

"You must have told me."

"I never told anyone."

Tracie held up her hands in surrender. "Okay. I found out about it. Years ago, when I visited you in Arlington before you met Bruno, I found your yearbook and read some of your notes. I thought it was so cute and I wanted to surprise you. I thought it'd be fun to see your face when you saw him again, so I looked him up. And when I found him, I met with him and he was wonderful. I didn't mean to fall in love with him, but that's what happened."

"I see."

"You'll find someone else, Anna Marie. It's only been a few months, you'll get over him. Can you forgive me?"

Anna Marie nearly laughed. How like Tracie. She'd taken her stockings and now Desmond, and she expected Anna Marie to forgive and forget. "Little sister, I don't even like you. But I realize that doesn't mean anything to you because you have a family and I've only been a footnote in your life. Now I'm going on with mine and I don't want you to be a part of it." She turned.

"But we're sisters."

"I know. But we're not friends."

Anna Marie pretended that she'd settled everything with Tracie as she rode back with Desmond to her house. But as he walked her to the front door she said, "There's something I have to tell you."

He swore. "I knew it. I felt that you were strangely quiet on the way back. What is it?"

"I can't see you anymore."

"Why not?"

"I think things have run their course." When he didn't say anything, she added, "Tracie really loves you."

"You know, it's funny, because somehow I'd convinced myself that *you* loved me."

"I do. I think I always have, but there are things about me that—"

"I can handle them. Do you really think that if we break up I'll go crawling back to Tracie? It won't happen. I'm not a toy or a pet that you can pass between the two of you."

"I know, but I have a past that's—"

He grabbed her shoulders. "I don't care."

"But what about your father?" she shot back. "You've worked so hard to get him to respect you. Do you want to start arguing with him again? I don't want you to ruin the relationship you have. It's very special. I know because I've never had one and I won't force you to choose."

"You mean you're afraid to." He released his hold. "It's okay, Anna Marie. You don't have to run away from me. You don't have to hide anything from me anymore. I'll let you go. You're free." His voice rose. "That's all you've ever wanted, right? To be free. Go ahead and run away. I won't stop you and I won't look for you," he said, then turned and left.

Anna Marie watched him go, her heart cracking. She went inside and saw her housemates' worried faces. They'd probably heard the shouting. She shook her head. "I can't talk right now." She started for the stairs, then stopped. She took a deep breath, turned around and went into the basement. She turned on the lights and saw the mirrors and the dance floor where Mrs. Bell had taught her how to dance and had given her all the tools to become Malika.

She saw an old radio and turned it on and began

to dance. She moved and spun, her sorrow, the feeling of loss growing. She let her tears stream down her face and didn't care. After a long while she fell to the floor and wept.

In her bedroom Anna Marie phoned Sonia, but couldn't reach her so she called Rania instead. "I wanted to let you know that I've broken the oath and lost a pair of stockings. I know it's over for me now."

"You lost a pair? That's a first. How did you do it?"

"I left them in a place in my bedroom where my sister found them and took them."

"Did she wear them?"

"Yes."

Rania laughed. "She won't wear them again, poor thing." Rania continued before Anna Marie could ask what she meant. "But that's not your problem. Do you consider your sister taking the stockings breaking the oath? Don't worry. We'll send you another pair."

"There's no point. I've had my dream come true and now I've woken up. I wanted to thank you and the society for my membership and for all that you've done. Besides, the magic is in the stockings, right? And I don't have my last pair."

"There's no magic, Anna Marie, and I think you're breaking the oath again. You're settling for less."

"No, I'm facing reality."

"And to you reality is always painful. People leave, dreams die."

"Yes."

"Do you think Sonia lives that way?"

"No, but—"

"She's no different than you. You deserve to be happy. You deserve to live with the man you love, but *you* have to decide that. We'll send you your last pair of stockings, but the rest is up to you."

The next day Anna Marie sat at the breakfast table dry-eyed and watched everyone eat. She was used to sadness, but never let it linger, because as a survivor, it had never done her any good.

She ate a few bites before setting her fork down. "I have something I want to say to you. I know who you really are. My sister told me about your past, but that doesn't matter to me. You don't need to worry about renewing your leases. As I promised, I will sign over the house to all three of you once the six months are completed."

"But we don't want the house," Gerald said.

"Yes, it's a big responsibility," Jane said.

"So you're leaving?" Leona said.

Anna Marie nodded. "If you don't want it, I'll have someone manage the place and yes, I'm leaving. I think it's time I go out on my own and see the world."

"You're not here by mistake," Gerald said. "Mrs. Bell knows things about people. Years ago I made a mistake. I'd been unemployed over a year and I needed money to take care of my family. I got a crazy idea with a friend of mine to rob a wealthy couple his wife worked for. They weren't supposed to be home when we got there, but they'd had a change of plans and everything went wrong from there. My friend always blamed me for leaving witnesses, but I'm not a killer at heart. I served my time and lost everything I'd tried to save—my family and my home. I met Mrs. Bell while working as a janitor in a club. I was living in a homeless shelter at the time and she gave me a place to stay."

"I thought you were retired."

"Mrs. Bell left us all some money to live on," Jane said. "That's the kind of woman she was. Her only stipulation was that we help others. So we go into town several times a week and volunteer with different organizations." Jane pulled a strand of her hair. "Mrs. Bell and I were friends from way back. I even knew her real name. She was older than I was, but we clicked instantly. I'd left my family to come to the city to be a star." She laughed with irony. "I ended up being on stage, but not the kind of stage I'd envisioned. However, it paid the bills and a drug habit I'd developed. I kicked it with her help. She saved my life. She took me in and made me feel whole again."

"Me, too," Leona said. "My husband was a bastard, but I depended on him. I wanted to make extra money so I got into the prescription drug trade. I got probation and instead of running back to my husband, I ran with nothing but the clothes on my back. I met Mrs. Bell at a bus stop. It was raining, I had nowhere else to go, she took me in and I never left."

"She knew we needed each other," Jane said. "You needed us as much as we needed you."

Gerald nodded. "And we thought you were happy here."

"I am," Anna Marie said in a quiet voice.

"What happened last night?" Jane said. "Did you and Desmond have a fight?"

"Of course, they had a fight," Gerald said. "We could hear them."

"I was just making sure."

"Yes, we had a fight," Anna Marie said. "You see, his father means a lot to him and his father would definitely not approve of me once he found out my history."

"What is there to learn?"

Anna Marie told them, despite the pain it cost her, because they'd been open and she felt they deserved the same. She told them everything—the foster homes, the men's clubs she'd worked in, the bad boyfriends, the bad associates and scores of poor choices. When she was done, Jane had tears running down her face, Gerald stared at the table and Leona shook her head in disbelief.

"So now you understand," Anna Marie said.

Leona sighed. "I think you're being unfair to Desmond. He's a strong man and he's not going to live his life just to please his father. You once said that you ran away from here. Why?"

"Well, I was about to turn eighteen and get out of the system and I knew the benefit payments would end, and that Mrs. Bell would never put me out. I didn't want to burden her, so I left."

"Why didn't you tell Mrs. Bell how you felt?"

"Because I knew she would feel guilty."

"No, you didn't know," Jane said. "That's what you guessed, but you guessed wrong."

"What?"

"Mrs. Bell wanted to adopt you. I only knew about you through her stories. She never mentioned your name, but she said you were the first and only foster child she wanted to adopt. She loved you, that's why she gave you this place. You can't know how someone really feels unless you talk to them. You're so used to being mistreated you think everyone's the same, but they're not. Give Desmond a chance. If he decides to leave because of his father, then he's not the man for you. But don't make decisions for him."

"And don't make a decision for us, either," Gerald said. "We don't want you to leave. We want you to stay as long as you want."

Jane nodded. "And if you do decide to move out, we want you close by so that you can visit."

Leona covered Anna Marie's hand. "We love you, my dear. Like family."

Anna Marie stared at them, touched. A family? Her heart filled with joy at the word. She had a family. People who cared about her, people to whom she could belong. She wasn't an outsider anymore. She no longer needed to run from her past. "I'll stay."

"Good," Gerald said. "Because we weren't going to let you leave."

"And you're not going to let Desmond go, either," Leona said.

Anna Marie let her shoulders sag. "But I don't know how to fix things."

"Be yourself."

She laughed. "I don't know how to."

"Yes, you do. Tell him everything."

Chapter 16

Anna Marie thought over her family's advice the rest of the day. She went into the basement to think some more and looked at the row of CDs Mrs. Bell had organized against a far wall. She looked at the space and remembered how Mrs. Bell had used dance to build her confidence. Now she could do the same, but not just for children. She would focus on teenage girls and women. Yes, she would make the classes affordable and fun. She could have a special course for wives who want to heat up their marriages.

"What do you think?" Anna Marie said aloud, not expecting an answer. She grabbed one of Mrs. Bell's favorite albums and opened the case. She stopped when she saw a small note with her name scrawled across it. She set the cover aside and read it.

Hello, Anna Marie,

   If you're reading this, then I know that you've done everything that I've asked of you. I hope that I've left you more than money and a house. I'll never know why you ran away, but I'm happy to know that you're now home. I imagine that you're the beautiful, talented young woman that I knew you would be. You've made an old woman's dream come true. I hope your dreams will come true, too. Don't be afraid to love, don't be afraid to hope. You can become what you imagine.
Love always, Mrs. Bell

Anna Marie squeezed her eyes shut and whispered, "Thank you." She opened her eyes and through a teary haze glanced around the bare studio and imagined all that she would do, and how she would make Mrs. Bell proud.

"Anna Marie?" Leona called from the top of the stairs. "Are you down there?"

Anna Marie wiped away her tears. "Yes."

"You have a phone call."

She started up the stairs. Could it be Desmond? Had he changed his mind about her?

Leona saw the look of expectation on her face and shook her head. "It's your sister."

"Oh." Anna Marie took the phone and went into the dining room. "Hello, Tracie," she said without feeling.

"What did you do to them?" her sister shrieked.

Anna Marie held the phone away from her ear. "What are you talking about?"

"The stockings! You did something to them just to get back at me."

"No, I didn't."

"Then why am I in bed covered in a nasty rash?"

Anna Marie hid a laugh. "I don't know."

"You did this to me to keep me away from Desmond. If this rash leaves a mark, I'll get you."

"Tracie, I didn't even know you were going to take the stockings. I told you to leave them, remember?"

"It's not fair," she screamed like a petulant child.

"No, it's not fair. It's not fair that you tried to force me to give up a man you don't really love. You only want him because he doesn't want you."

Tracie fell silent, then said, "He used to talk about you. He couldn't remember your name, but he'd tell me about this girl he'd known at some halfway house he'd gone to. And I wanted him to think about me."

"At least his parents love you."

"It's not the same."

"Why him? Of all the men, Tracie, why did you choose him?"

"Just to see if I could get what you couldn't. It was a nice challenge at first, but then I fell in love with him. I slept with the other man just to get back at him. I wanted him to notice me. At that point in our marriage, I felt he'd only married me to impress his parents and once I'd fulfilled that, he didn't have much use for me. He didn't love me the way I wanted him to."

"I'm going to see him again."

Tracie sighed. "I thought you might and I know when I'm beaten. I'll find someone else to adore me."

"Yes, you always do," Anna Marie said, then she wished her sister a speedy recovery and hung up. A package arrived the next day. She opened it and pulled out a pair of full-body stockings and knew exactly what she had to do.

"Look, I know she's no Malika," Julius said, staring at the agile young woman on the stage, "but you could at least pretend you're enjoying yourself."

Desmond finished his drink. He knew it wasn't his first, but had stopped counting after three. He shouldn't have let Advent persuade him to come back here. The Palace of Sin held too many memories for him. It filled him with a feeling of loss that no amount of alcohol could fill, which didn't mean he wouldn't stop trying. He raised his hand to the waitress for another refill.

Julius frowned. "I know you can drink me under the table, but you should go easy on those."

Desmond picked up his glass. "This was a bad idea."

"You thought that the last time, but you had fun. I'm trying to cheer you up."

"I don't need cheering up."

"I've never seen you fall this hard for a woman. What's gotten into you?"

Desmond thanked the waitress when she set down his drink. He took a long swallow.

"Call her."

Desmond stared at the liquid in his glass. "I told you it's over."

"So you had a fight. You can always make up."

"Not this time. I'm not calling her and she won't call me."

Suddenly his cell phone vibrated. He glanced down and noticed the number. He blinked. "I don't believe it." He abruptly left the table and Julius watched him leave, then sat back and returned his gaze to the dancer, ready to enjoy the show.

Anna Marie entered the law office of Thornberg and West, remembering the first time she'd arrived and how unsure and alone she had felt. She didn't feel that way now. She walked up to the reception-ist ready to announce who she was there to see, when the woman smiled and said, "Go right in, Ms.

Williams. He told me to let you through the moment you arrived."

"Thank you."

Anna Marie walked back to Desmond's office, grateful that he'd agreed to see her, although his voice had been distant over the phone. She took a deep breath, knocked, then opened the door when he responded. Desmond sat at his desk looking agitated. Before she lost her courage she spoke.

"I'm sorry about everything and you were right. No, please don't say anything. Let me finish. It's important I tell you this."

Desmond frowned and opened his mouth, but she rushed ahead before he could speak.

"I shouldn't have kept secrets from you and I won't keep them from you anymore." She opened her coat then let it drop to the ground to reveal the harem outfit she'd worn the night of her performance. The full-body stockings she wore added a sensuous tint to her skin tone. "I know I should have told you who I was before, but I couldn't. I was afraid of what you'd say. That night in the club, I *did* dance for you. Everything I said *was* for you. But I have danced for other men and my past is shady, which I won't go into right now. But if you'll give me another chance, I'll tell you."

Desmond covered his eyes as though he were in pain. "Will you excuse us?"

Anna Marie wasn't sure what he meant until she saw him glance to his left. She turned and saw his parents sitting on the couch, stunned.

She looked at Desmond in panic ready to run.

"It's okay," Desmond said.

"No, it's not okay," his father said. "This is the woman you took to our church bazaar? The one you introduced to us as a good woman? You met her in a club?"

"Yes."

"Of adult entertainment?"

"Yes."

Pastor Rockwell turned to Anna Marie. "Do you know what sin is?"

Desmond smiled. "Yes, that's where she danced. The Palace of Sin, right?"

Anna Marie nodded, still unable to speak.

"Good. I wanted to make sure of the name."

"You shouldn't have been there at all," his father said.

Mrs. Rockwell spoke up. "My dear, you look chilly. Perhaps you should put your coat back on."

Anna Marie picked up her coat. "I don't dance anymore."

Pastor Rockwell stood. "Come, Mother, we're leaving."

"That's another thing Desmond and I have in common. I wasn't good enough for my father, either."

Pastor Rockwell spun around and gaped at her.

"What do you mean by that? I'm an excellent father. You were placed in foster homes because your parents weren't suitable."

"No, they weren't. My father had all the appearance of goodness, but his heart was cold. He rejected me because I wasn't good enough for him. No one was good enough for him. Not my sister, my mother and definitely not me. Rejection comes in many forms and I've seen them all. Don't do the same." She touched his sleeve. "Please don't leave like this. I may not be like Tracie, but I do love your son. I will never betray him. I will always be true to him."

"I prefer Anna Marie to her sister," Desmond said.

"Who's her sister?" Pastor Rockwell asked.

"Your ex-daughter-in-law," Desmond responded.

"Tracie?" Pastor Rockwell looked at him, startled. "She never told us she had a sister."

"Tracie didn't tell us a lot of things. She's a good liar. That's one of the reasons I divorced her."

Pastor Rockwell pressed a hand to his forehead. "I still can't approve of this match." His gaze fell to Anna Marie. "I'm sorry."

"I'm also quitting law to restructure Hallon House," Desmond said. "I spoke to the owners and they want to partner with me."

"You want to leave all this?" He gestured to the fine room and furnishings. "All that you've worked for? I don't understand you."

"You never did, but I don't need you to understand or approve. I don't need you to be my pastor or my teacher or my judge. Just my father. That's all."

Pastor Rockwell opened his mouth to argue, then stopped and sighed, resigned. "Very well. You've always done your own thing anyway. You've never cared what I think."

Anna Marie shook her head. "No, he does care and I care, too, but we won't be slaves to your opinion. That's the difference."

Mrs. Rockwell took her husband's arm. "I think enough has been said for now. Let's leave them alone."

He cast a glance at his son, then nodded and left.

Anna Marie turned to Desmond. "I'm sorry that—"

"Don't worry." Desmond shut the door, then led Anna Marie to the couch and they both sat. "You certainly know how to make an impression."

Her cheeks burned in humiliation. "I didn't know they'd be here."

"Neither did I." He rested his arm on her shoulders. "But I'm glad."

"You don't seem very surprised that I'm Malika."

"I'm not."

She stared at him. "You knew?"

"Of course. Not at first, but as time went on, I picked up the clues."

"Why didn't you say anything? When Tracie hinted at it, I thought you didn't know."

"I was waiting for you to tell me. I wanted to see if you trusted me, but after that day, I knew you didn't."

"I know," she said, ashamed.

Desmond stood and opened a desk drawer. "Fortunately, I forgive you." He pulled out a gift and handed it to her.

"What's this for?"

He shoved his hands in his pockets. "Just open it."

Anna Marie carefully tore back the wrapping paper, then gasped and ripped with more vigor until the item was visible. "'One Thousand and One Nights.' Fully illustrated with gold-leaf trim." Anna Marie held it close to her chest and stared up at Desmond with tears gleaming in her eyes. "Thank you." She lowered her gaze and ran her hand over the cover, then rested the book on her lap and flipped through its pages. "It's even better than I remembered," she whispered. She turned a page, then noticed a ring tucked in the spine. "What is this?"

Desmond picked up the ring, then got down on one knee. His gaze pierced hers, but his voice remained soft. "I hope it's a dream come true." He lifted her hand and placed the ring on her finger. "Will you marry me?"

Anna Marie pushed the book off her lap and

threw her arms around him. "Yes. A hundred times yes. I can't believe it."

Desmond held her tight. "Believe it, darling, because it's real. I love you."

She closed her eyes and sighed. "I love you, too. More than you know."

Chapter 17

Anna Marie never thought she'd return to The Palace of Sin, but she wanted to see Belinda again and tell her about Desmond and the dance studio she was starting.

"She's not here anymore," Fred told her when Anna Marie asked him. "She left about a month after you. I had to scramble to get a replacement."

"Was she in any kind of trouble?" Anna Marie asked worriedly.

"No, she said she had a new opportunity some-where in Nevada. She wasn't more specific than that." He snapped his fingers, remembering some-thing. "But she left you an envelope. I was going to post it, but since you're here…" He disappeared into his office, then returned with it.

"Thank you," Anna Marie said, surprised by its weight.

Fred crossed his arms. "Is there any way I can convince you to come back?"

Anna Marie glanced around the empty executive lounge with its Eastern decor and shook her head. "No, those days are definitely over for me."

"I understand." He nodded, then left.

Anna Marie opened the envelope and read the brief note:

Hope you finally got what you deserved and that this gift will help you remember me.

Anna Marie pulled out a keychain in the shape of a stocking. She laughed, then gripped the key chain in her fist. "Oh, Belinda," she said aloud. "I'll always remember you." She kissed the key chain, then ran outside. She blinked as her eyes adjusted to the bright fall sunlight. Her gaze fell on Desmond as he leaned against his motorcycle, looking both sexy and dangerous in his leather jacket and dark sunglasses. Her heart leaped at the sight of him. He was no longer a mysterious figure who would disappear like a dream. Her dream had come true.

Desmond straightened when he saw her and removed his sunglasses. "Is everything okay?"

"Yes, everything is wonderful." She threw her arms around him, her heart filled with joy. "I love you."

He drew back and his eyes melted into hers. "I love you, too."

"And I want to spend the rest of my life with you."

Desmond kissed her, then whispered words she'd always wanted to hear. "Your wish is my command."

HELP CELEBRATE
ARABESQUE'S
15TH ANNIVERSARY!

2009 marks Arabesque's 15th anniversary!

Help us celebrate by telling us about your most special memories and moments with Arabesque books. Entries will be judged by the Arabesque Anniversary Committee based on which are the most touching and well written. Fifteen lucky winners will receive as a prize a full-grain leather duffel bag with the Arabesque anniversary logo.